A SKETCH AWAY FROM PERFECT

The Art of Having It All

Book 1

SADIE WATERS

ROGUE WOLF PUBLISHING

For Kinley. Thanks for saving me.

Contents

ONE

Embarrassing Realities

Harper

"You should totally do it. My sister made loads of money. I think she paid off *all* her student loans!" McKenzy says, tapping the 'Apply' button on the screen insistently.

I look at https://atalooseend.com like it's a snake that's going to bite me. How did it come to this?!

"You're a poor, starving artist who doesn't sell enough pieces to cover the rent," she answers my unspoken question, her tone flat. "You have student loans so far up your ass you can taste the red ink! Trust me, this is your best option."

"But… what if they want sex?" I question, wondering if I have it in me to become an escort. I've never done anything like that before, though I'm certainly not a virgin.

McKenzy stabs her finger at the bold, red, 64-font words on the 'About' page. "'Dates are NOT required to or encouraged to provide sex or engage in sexual acts'. It's even in the legalese we read in the sample contract. Big and bold. In fact, if we go to the home page…" She reaches over my shoulder and maneuvers on my touchpad. "Ah, yes. See? They've practically got a neon sign with flares going off around it."

I have to admit, the website is making that point abundantly clear. "Still, dating for money? Isn't that a bit, you know, whorish?"

"Honey," she says, "you're at the end of your options. You're a beautiful, sophisticated, twenty-five-year-old starving artist. Shake that booty. Shake it now."

Then she hip-checks me out of the way of my own laptop and stabs my touchpad, lighting up the 'Apply' button.

"I'll just fill this out for you, if you're too nervous. Or proud." She winks at me. "You know, you're far too stuffy for a sexy woman your age. Live a little. Just give me your social security number and payment info when I ask for it, and you'll be all set."

I sit down on a plastic-and-metal chair creation of McKenzy's and try not to let out my internal scream. But she was right. If I'm going to stand on my own two feet and stop asking my parents for money, this is how it has to be.

"How's the 'rents?" she asks.

I swear she's a mind reader. "Pissed. They said if I ask for rent money one more time, they're moving me home, whether I want to go or not."

"Daaaaaamn." She fills out a few more fields.

I lean forward. "Just what the heck did you put in the 'interests' box?!"

"Big dicks." McKenzy rolls her eyes. "Relax. Art. Nature. Long walks on the beach. A good book. Partying—"

"I don't enjoy partying. I haven't done that since college," I object.

"Yeah, but they don't need to know that," she replies. "I mean, you're going to be a rent-a-woman. You're supposed to sound like you're a good time."

I groan. "McKenzy…"

"Relax. I've got this. You just go finish that painting you've been putting the 'finishing touches' on for a month." I can hear the condescension in her tone.

"You once wrestled with a coffee table design for the better part of a year," I protest.

"That was different. With the model, I can make more than one of its kind."

I see her type 'sexy and single' in another box and want to throttle her. Instead, I look away and respond to our conversation. "What do you think a lithograph print is?"

"Yeah, yeah. It's never the same as having the original," she mutters. "Okay, social security and payment info."

Thinking about my debts and knowing I've been utterly defeated, I sigh out the number. "And the email address for my payment method is michaelvernonfan33@gmail.com."

McKenzy swings her head around. "Are you still crushing on that guy?"

"I'm not! McKenzy, he's my favorite artist. I'm not crushing on him. I admire him and his work," I explain with failing patience.

"I get you. I get you. But I'll bet you'd pose naked for him and then roll around in the paint if you could." She giggles.

I rub my temples. "He's married."

"Well, shit. There goes a perfectly good fantasy," she laments.

"Are you done yet?"

McKenzy cracks her knuckles. "Aaaaand 'Submit.' Congratulations, you're a registered escort."

I throw a fuzzy decorative pillow at her. "Date. I'm a date!"

"I know. I'm just messing with you." She steps away from my laptop humming, proud of herself.

I feel sick to my stomach, nervously going over to see the profile she's made. "McKenzy, this isn't me!"

"Of course it's not you," she replies. "It's the you that you need to be to hook a man."

The profile picture in particular mortifies me. "I am *not* using a beach shot in a bikini as my picture!"

"You should actually add a lot more pictures," she muses. "They'll want to see you from every angle."

I consider shutting the whole thing down right then and there, but then my banking app pings my phone to tell me my balance has reached zero dollars.

"I'm changing the profile pic," I grumble. I look at my phone again and wince as the bank app continues with another push notif-ication, letting me know something bounced. "And… maybe add a few more."

McKenzy claps me on the back. "That's the spirit!"

* * *

TWO HOURS LATER, I've got what I think is a profile I can live with, sans bikini pics. I am just drying my hair after showering off flecks of paint, when my laptop dings. Curious, I look at my phone then realize I haven't downloaded the At a Loose End app. It has to be the app. Everything else is synced to my phone.

I cautiously flip my laptop open, almost afraid the website will suck me in and deposit me at the feet of some pervert. Taking several deep breaths, I remind myself that I get the final say on who I choose to "date."

My avatar in the upper right corner winks playfully at me, tempting me to look at the request.

I have no choice. It's this or move back to Otsego to live with my parents. There is no *way* I'm moving back home..

I click on my avatar, and the very helpful drop-down shows me I have one request—and a message. I think I can handle the message. Actually, accepting the request might require some huffing into a paper bag first.

ScottIAm: Hi.

'Hi'? That's all I get? I look at his avatar, an ear of corn, and see a green dot indicating he's online. I decide to respond. If I can feel him out, maybe I'll feel better about accepting the date.

ArtIsMyLife33: Hi. I'm Harper. ~~This is actually my first time~~

Oh, right, let's start with that, Harper. Great start there. I shake my head at myself. At least I didn't embarrass myself right off the bat.

ArtIsMyLife33: Hi. I'm Harper. ~~Are you interested in a date?~~

Would you like to chop me up into little bits in your van? Ugh. Get it together, girl!

ArtIsMyLife33: Hi. I'm Harper. ~~I hear you need a date.~~

I bang my head on my screen, causing the touch screen to get mad and try to minimize everything. *No, Harper, he's contacting you because he needs advice on how to make a casserole.* I restore my Internet window.

ArtIsMyLife33: Hi. I'm Harper.

Enter.

Done.

…

Fuck.

ScottIAm: …

ScottIAm: Hi, Harper. I'm Scott. Pleased to meet you.

What am I supposed to say to that? 'Pleased to meet you too'? I'm not exactly pleased. I'm desperate.

ArtIsMyLife33: ~~Listen, I'm here for your wallet, you're here for my arm candy, let's just get this over w~~

I take a deep breath through my nose and let it slowly out of my mouth. I need to feel this guy out because, as much as I don't want to move back to Otsego, I want to end up being pulled from the Mississippi in pieces even less.

ScottIAm: This is kind of awkward, isn't it?

Yeah, no shit.

ArtIsMyLife33: Yeah, it kinda is.

ScottIAm: Your profile says I'd be your first date. You just started today? I'm not being creepy, I swear. I'm just curious about… you know… why.

Isn't that the million-dollar question. Actually, I'd happily settle for a couple of thousand to resuscitate my bank account. I can hear it panting from here.

ArtIsMyLife33: 25-year-old starving artist. No great mystery there, I guess.

ScottIAm: You're really an artist? That's cool. I'm an organic farmer. I don't know if you looked at my request yet, but I'm completely vetted, and I promise I've had all my shots, and I don't bite. What kind of art do you do? That's not in your profile, and I don't see any pictures.

ArtIsMyLife33: My friend made my profile. I was too chicken, to be completely honest with you. If we hit it off, I'd love to talk to you about my art. You would be my first date. I know it probably says in the request, but where do you need me to go and why?

ScottIAm: Cousin's wedding this Friday. I'm trying to keep my family off my back about marriage, so I need a stand-in girlfriend. Can I see some of your art? I'm really curious now.

I eye the expectant little chat bar with its seductive plus sign for adding photographs. *What the hell? I'm an artist. I should be happy to exhibit my art wherever to whomever!* I click the plus sign and attach a high-quality image of one of my paintings.

ScottIAm: That's beautiful. Have you sold it already?

I wish. I open the image and stare despondently at my colorful, abstract oil painting of a lake scene.

ArtIsMyLife33: No bites yet.

ScottIAm: I lied. Maybe I do bite.

I laugh.

ArtIsMyLife33: LOL, seriously, I don't expect you to buy my artwork in order to get me to be your stand-in girlfriend. But thanks for saying it's beautiful.

ScottIAm: Is this where I should drop the line, "But not as beautiful as you"?

I laugh harder. I am starting to like this guy.

ArtIsMyLife33: You want some crackers with that cheese?

ScottIAm: Lol. So, would you consider giving this a try? It's my first time too. I figure we can help each other through it.

My fingers hover over the keys. Then, I make a decision.

ArtIsMyLife33: Yeah. Let's give this a try.

ScottIAm: Great! So, I think you just accept my request or something, but do you know where you'd like to meet so I can pick you up? I don't want you to feel like I'm stalking your address.

With a snort, I give it some thought.

ArtIsMyLife33: Let's meet at the Hampden Co-Op. It's not far from where I live.

ScottIAm: Sounds great. Pick you up at 11:00 AM?

ArtIsMyLife33: Sounds great. But Scott, one thing. If you chop me up and throw me in the Mississippi, I am going to haunt you for all eternity.

ScottIAm: Lol! Same, Harper. Same.

Then Scott signs off, his green dot going a vacant white. I sit back in my chair, feeling stunned but also a bit relieved. It seems like my first date is actually going to be okay.

I pull up Scott's profile, just to double-check before I pull the trigger and Lord, have mercy. I do a double-take at his profile pic. How can a man that handsome have to *buy* a date to stand in at his cousin's wedding?! Chestnut brown hair, sky blue eyes, boyish grin, and the cutest dimples I've ever seen!

After giving it some thought, I decide that's probably exactly why he's hiring me. He doesn't want any weird set-ups by family members trying to marry him off. With me, there's no chance of any messy romantic entanglements.

No chance at all.

TWO

Farmer Scott

Harper

I try not to pull a Marilyn Monroe as the wind whips the flared skirt of the sleeveless aquamarine dress I am wearing. McKenzy loaned me a pair of high-heeled, strappy sandals to match, and they aren't helping the situation much as I teeter along the sidewalk, expecting to be swept away like Mary Poppins.

As I turn the corner onto Raymond Avenue, I pause to adjust one of the straps on the right sandal.

"I should have worn tennis shoes," I grumble, even though I know that wouldn't be appropriate. It's my own fault for losing one of my own silver slippers. Not in a Cinderella way, but in a this-closet-is-an-unholy-vortex way. I'm sure, when I finally get around to cleaning it, the missing slipper will reappear. .

"Yeah, when I'm being moved to a nursing home," I mutter. I catch my reflection in one of the storefront windows and pat back a strand of my hair. At least that's clipped up in a twist so the wind can only do so much damage.

In the reflection, I also see a police car. I swear the side says Otsego.I spin around, but the car is already speeding down the block.

"That's bizarre." I think of my ex-boyfriend, Jack Collins, for a second or two. He's an Otsego cop, but Otsego is forty minutes away from St. Paul. I shake my head. "Pretty soon here, I'm going to need a tinfoil hat."

"It'd match the shoes," a low voice chuckles.

I look up and straight into the warmest blue eyes I've ever seen in my life. I smile when I recognize it's my date–Scott.

"Uh, hi," I say, embarrassed about being caught talking to myself.

He sticks out his hand. "Hi. I'm Scott Bauer."

Sheepishly, I shake it. "Harper Ward."

"I could get you a tinfoil hat, if you like." Scott grins. "It'd make a real statement at the wedding."

"A statement like 'look who showed up with crazy'?" I smile back.

"Hey, as long as I show up with somebody, it'll be fine." Scott offers me his arm. "Since you're about to fly away any minute now, I figure you'd better hang onto me while we walk to the coffee shop."

I look down at my skirt, which is already trying to get tangled around a lamppost. "Yeah, good plan."

Surprisingly, Scott leads the way. I eye him suspiciously. "You researched the area before, didn't you?"

"Yes," Scott admits with a grin. "I'll bet I even know where you live."

"Is it that obvious?" I laugh.

"You're an artist. Carleton Artist Lofts is nearby. It just seems to make sense. Am I wrong?" Scott asks. We enter the coffee shop, and I get a strong whiff of ground beans.

I chuckle. "And here I thought I was being so stealthy."

Scott pulls out a chair for me at one of the pleasantly beat-up tables. "Don't worry about it. I moonlight as an amateur detective."

"No, you don't," I snort.

His dimples deepen as his smile widens. "No, I don't. But I'm not going to give you too much crap over it. I think you've learned your lesson. And since I'm not the Mississippi River Slasher, you don't need to worry. Just, maybe, pick somewhere a little further away from home for a meeting point next time, yeah?" His beautiful blue eyes are genuinely concerned.

"Point taken," I agree.

"So," he says without sitting down. "What can I get you?"

"A London Fog would be great, thanks. But you don't have to buy me coffee. I mean…" I feel my cheeks heat up.

Scott winks. "Let me buy myself into your good graces. I figure we could at least get to know each other a bit before I sweep you off to the wedding."

"Okay." I relent. I mean, what else am I going to do?

Scott goes to the counter and comes back with my London Fog and a drink for himself. He sits across from me, sipping what I can only imagine is *very* strong coffee, from the fragrance.

"Tall, black coffee?" I guess.

"Got it in one. Didn't know you were a psychic too. Is that what you're doing on those 'long walks on the beach'?" Scott teases me.

I groan and drop my head on my arm. "Don't remind me. Tell me she took out the partying bit?"

"I could kind of tell from the profile pic you chose that you weren't the 'party girl' your friend made you out to be. Not that you don't enjoy a good time, but most of the 'party girls' on that site are holding a beer in one hand and a cropped-out ex in the other," Scott laughs.

"Oh, God." I peek up at Scott. "I'm not a crazy cat lady. I swear. I don't even have a cat."

"You're not a crazy cat lady *yet*," Scott corrects me. "And I like that about you."

I pull out my phone to check my profile. "She didn't seriously put that in there…"

He puts a hand over mine. "No. That was a personal observation. I think you're a hard worker, like me, and serious about your success, so you don't go out making *Girls Gone Wild* videos and drinking until you're dancing topless on tables. You're just the kind of girl I want." A charming blush creeps into his tan cheeks. "I mean, as a date." A cough. "To my cousin's wedding."

I smile at him and put my phone away. "You won't see this again for the rest of the night. I just had to make sure McKenzy didn't go totally wild. She has the login, you know? She could do anything. She wanted to make my profile pic a bikini shot!"

"That would have been nice," he admits. "But not what I was looking for. I was looking for you."

I feel all warm and fuzzy inside. We stare at each other for a long moment, something magnetic happening between us.

Then Scott clears his throat. "We should probably go to that wedding."

"Yeah, probably." I start to stand, but Scott rushes to pull out my chair for me. He's attractive, and a gentleman. I am so doomed. "Hey, Scott?" I say as he offers me his arm again.

"Hey, Harper?" he echoes with twinkling eyes.

"Would it be out of line for me to say I wish we weren't going to a wedding, and this was a real date?"

Scott's eyes soften. "No," he replies. "You wouldn't be out of line at all."

* * *

SCOTT

Holy fuck, this woman is hot!

I'm tempted to tell my cousin my truck broke down and take Harper to some fancy Minneapolis restaurant. One of the ones with the cloth napkins and champagne I would feel completely out of place in. It would be nothing like the farm, but for Harper, it would be worth it.

I give myself a mental shake. If I don't go to that wedding, I will never hear the end of it and I need Harper to be my shield. So, no cloth napkins for us,, not tonight, at least. Still, it's hard to focus on going back out to the church in Vermillion and later dancing at The Wexford at the Emerald Greens Golf Course.

Dancing. I feel the warmth of Harper's hand through my light jacket, and I'm glad I'm not wearing a tie, just a nice white shirt. If

I had been wearing a tie, I wouldn't be able to breathe. *She smells like lilacs.*

I am in so much trouble.

Harper is strawberry blonde with long hair that curls in soft waves, begging to be wrapped around a man's wrist. Her eyes match her dress perfectly, a cheerful aquamarine. With a smoking body and the cutest little sprinkling of pale freckles across her nose, there is no doubt in my mind she would be incredible in bed—but that's not why we're here, I remind myself.

"She Thinks My Tractor's Sexy" begins playing in my head on a loop, and it's all I can do not to snicker at my stupid thoughts. Though I can see Harper riding my tractor, perched right in my lap. Suddenly, my pants feel a little too tight.

Luckily, my workhorse of a Ford F-450 Super Duty King Ranch comes into view, huge compared to the city folks' cars parked along the street in front of and behind it. I'd given her a good washing before coming to get Harper, but there is still a little bit of dirt clinging to the mud flaps.

Harper gives a low whistle. "Is that yours?" she asks, pointing right at Big Bertha.

"She sure is," I reply proudly. I unlock the truck and swing open the passenger door. "Watch your step," I say, helping her up. For all the times my mom asks me why I don't get around to putting running boards on Big Bertha, I can finally tell her. It's because one day, I was meant to put my hands on Harper's waist and lift her into my truck.

"Thanks," Harper says. The most adorable blush touches her cheeks, making those cute little freckles stand out even more.

"Any time. Seriously, *any* time," I respond. My voice is more growly than usual. I probably look like a horny teenager. Hell, I *feel* like a horny teenager.

"I think we're supposed to go to the wedding now," Harper murmurs throatily, and it goes all the way to my groin.

It also means I've been caught staring. "Right." I close the door, careful not to catch her dress, and run around to the other side of the truck.

I get in, throw the truck in gear, and squeeze out of the parking spot. Two idiot sedan drivers gave me a couple of inches on each bumper. Stupid city folk. Maybe you could get a Smart Car out of here without a problem, but this is gonna be tight.

"That was impressive," Harper remarks when I finally ease Big Bertha free. She puts a hand on my knee.

I show all my great driving skill by almost rear-ending a Cadillac. "Thanks." I gulp.

"Sorry," Harper says, starting to remove her hand. "I shouldn't have—"

I grab her hand and put it back right where it was. "You definitely should have. Just give a man a little warning next time. It's not every day I get a sexy woman groping my thigh." I grin so she knows it's a joke.

"Oh, Scott, if I was groping your thigh, you'd know it," Harper shoots back.

Her wit is going to be the death of me. Sure, she's hot, but this easy banter between us is something I've never had before. "I'm sure I would."

I hold Harper's hand in my lap all the way to Vermillion, not minding the forty-minute drive one bit this time. The church rises tall and beautiful on one of the main drags. I'm tempted to drive right past it and into a cornfield. I'm willing to bet Harper will show me what it really means to grope my thigh if I do.

Focus. Janet's wedding. Janet's wedding! I force myself to imagine the chewing-out I'll get from my mother if I don't attend.

Reluctantly, I park near the church and go to help Harper out of the truck. She slides all the way down my body as I pull her out and set her on her feet.

"Holy fuck," I groan. I'm sure Harper can feel the problem between us.

Harper bites her lip. "Maybe I should stand in front of you for a minute while you convince your friend it's a bad time to make an appearance."

"Yeah, I think that'd be a good idea," I agree. But I still have to move her a couple of inches away from my body, or the problem's never gonna go away.

"So, what's organic farming like?" Harper asks.

I smile at her, knowing she's trying to help. "It's hard, but worth it."

Harper glances down at the word 'hard,' and I have to laugh.

"I like hard things," she mumbles.

THREE

Hard But Worth It

Harper

Okay. You can do this. I throw my shoulders back and walk on Scott's arm, exuding confidence. At least, I think I'm exuding confidence. I've never been anybody's fake date before.

"You don't have to smile like that. Your face will break in half," he whispers to me, his arm shaking with repressed laughter.

Okay, so, not so confident then. I'm a little embarrassed, but I think my smile's genuine now. "I don't want to screw this up for you," I confess.

"If you do, you can make it up to me by letting me buy you dinner sometime," he murmurs back.

My spirits perk up at that possibility. I mean, the chemistry between us is undeniable. "How about, if I screw up, *I* buy *you* dinner, and if I knock it out of the park, you can buy me dinner?"

Scott engulfs my hand with his warm, rough palm. "Works for me."

When we enter the church, a gray-haired woman in a floral dress spots us and rushes over. "Scott! Thank heavens. I was almost afraid you'd miss the wedding!"

"Mom, I'm still fifteen minutes early," he replies with a chuckle.

"Yes, well, you're just lucky the family pictures are after the service, young man," she says, shaking her finger at him. Then she spots me. "Oh my, is this her?"

He lets go of my hand to slide his arm around my waist, tucking me into his side. "This is her."

"Oh, my dear, you are lovely." His mother takes my hands in hers. "Scott's been awfully secretive about you. He says you've been dating for months, but does he introduce you to his mother? Hmph. He hasn't even told us your name!"

"Harper," I say, giving him the side-eye. It'd have been nice to be prepared for this scenario but I smile anyway. "It's my fault. I didn't want to meet the family until we were sure things were serious." *Take that, Scott Bauer!*

He has a coughing fit.

"Oh, dear, you're not getting sick, are you?" His mother puts her hand to his forehead, though it requires the diminutive woman to go all the way up on her tip-toes.

"I'm fine, Mom. Wrong tube, that's all," he says.

"Well, take a lozenge just the same. It has Vitamin C." She fishes in her clutch and pulls out a cough drop.

He takes it and starts to put it in his pocket, but she clucks her tongue at him. "It's not going to do a lot of good in there."

"Here," I chime in, taking the lozenge from him. "Let me help." I unwrap it and pop it between his surprised lips.

His mother beams. "What a sweet girl you are. Please, call me Marjory."

"Marjory, it's such a pleasure to meet you," I respond. "Seeing what a nice person you are now, I wish I'd asked him to introduce us sooner!"

She blushes. "You're such a dear. All right, let's get ourselves seated."

One of the two ushers shows us to a pew on the bride's side. As we sit down, Scott begins to crunch down on the lozenge.

His mother rolls her eyes. "Scott, dearest, what good is it going to do if you don't suck on it?" She dives into her purse again.

"Yes, honey, what good is it going to do if you don't suck on it?" I ask innocently.

He chokes for real this time.

The man next to Marjory, who I assume is Scott's father, reaches over and pounds him on the back. "Swallow, *then* breathe, son."

Scott's eyes are streaming, but he manages a nod.

Marjory comes up with another lozenge. "Here you are, dearest. This time, suck on it. It doesn't work unless you suck on it until it's done."

A thousand dirty thoughts cross my mind, and I'm sure all of them are reflecting in my eyes as Scott takes the new lozenge. He ends his last cough on a gulp, then pops the lozenge in his mouth.

"Remember," I tease in his ear. "You have to suck on it until it's 'done.'"

"I am so getting you back for this," he murmurs, the lozenge clicking against his teeth.

"I'm looking forward to it." I grin.

The music starts, and we put our friendly war aside. For now.

I expected the ceremony would be beautiful. I didn't expect to get teary-eyed at the I do's, but hell, I'm an artist. Sometimes things just affect me.

"Oh, my dear, here you go," Marjory says between her own sobs, handing me a tissue.

I dab my eyes. Scott squeezes my hand, giving me the most tender look. At least he doesn't think I'm hamming it up. I like that he knows I'm being sincere.

After the bride and groom kiss and make their way down the aisle, we all start filtering out, passing through the receiving line. I get to Scott's cousin Janet, the bride, and she stops me, gripping my hand. "You're Scott's girlfriend, aren't you?"

"Yes," I reply, nervously watching the guests build up behind me. "I'm Harper."

"I'm Janet. Well, you probably know that already. I love your dress," she says, looking me up and down. "You are so pretty!"

"Not as pretty as you. You look amazing," I gush back. A bride should always be the prettiest one around on her wedding day.

She smiles, making her look positively radiant. "It took hours. But I think I turned out all right. You've been dating Scott for a few months, right?"

The line has become a traffic jam behind me. "Yeah, a few months. Um… shouldn't you be greeting the other guests? I don't want to be a bother."

"Pfft. They can wait. It's *my* wedding day." She winks at me. "Scott never told me what you do. Are you a student? You look awfully young. Scott is thirty-one, you know?"

"Uh, I'm older than I look. Twenty-five," I reply. "I have a Master's degree and everything. I'm an artist. Mostly, I work in oil paint."

Janet squeals. "That is so cool!"

"Janet," Scott interjects. "You really do have to greet the other guests before they start to mutiny."

She huffs at him but finally lets go of my hand. "We'll talk later," she promises me.

"Sure, sounds great." I let Scott hustle me along through the rest of the line and out to his pick-up.

"My family really likes you." He smiles at me.

"Yeah, thanks for the heads up," I snort.

He blushes. "Sorry. I forgot to tell you."

"Big thing to miss." I give him an evil smile. "Did you suck on it until it was 'done'?"

"Oh, baby," he purrs back as he starts the truck. "I'm just getting started." He winks at me, and my stomach tightens into a ball of fire.

Oh my.

* * *

SCOTT

I've never been as bold in my life as I am with Harper. That lozenge banter was something I don't know whether to thank or curse my mother for because, not only am I thinking about things I could be sucking on instead of a lozenge, but I'm thinking about things Harper could be sucking on as well. Fuck, there is nothing I'd like better than tangling my hand in that ocean of rose gold waves while she bobs up and down on my dick.

"Problem again?" Harper asks innocently as we pull into the parking lot for the Wexford at Emerald Greens Golf Course.

I look down at the bulge in my pants and shrug, trying to be nonchalant. "Guess so."

"I guess I'm leaving you in the truck then," she teases, starting to open her door.

I reach across her to close it. The scent of lilacs tickles my nose and does not help my situation one bit. "You really want to go in there without me? My family will be all over you."

Harper taps her chin as though she's considering it.

"Please," I beg. "Don't leave me here like this."

"I won't. I was just kidding," she replies. She looks down at my bulge again.

"Harper, that's not helping." I sigh.

"Sorry." She looks out the window as the other guests get out of their cars and head into the venue. "We can't stay out here forever. Can't you think of granny panties or something?"

"Even if you were wearing granny panties, I'd still want you," I murmur, knowing I'm being too forward but not able to stop myself.

She smiles at me, which only makes the situation worse. Then she starts fumbling in her purse.

"Please don't be going for a lozenge," I groan.

"I'm not." Instead, Harper pulls out a sealed packet of tissues.

I raise an eyebrow. "What's that for? Are you afraid the reception's going to get to you too?"

"It probably will," she replies. "But that's not what I'm pulling them out for." She peels open the packet and pulls out three tissues.

"What are you…?" I ask, then trail off. "Harper, if you're thinking of helping me out, you have to know, you really don't have to do that."

She flashes me a coy smile. "I know I don't have to, and I don't want you to think I'm some sort of a slut who usually does shit like this on the first date. But you and I have a connection, don't we?" She sets the tissues aside.

I nod, unable to speak at the moment as her tongue darts out and wets her bottom lip.

"Well, then, Scott, if you're willing, I'm happy to help you out."

"Okay..." I manage to verbalize. My eyes just about bugging out of my head as Harper reaches over and unzips my pants.

"Damn, this problem is bigger than I thought," she mumbles, fishing my dick out of my boxers.

I can't breathe. "Shit!"

Harper grips my cock and starts stroking it from base to tip. At first, I manage to take a look around the parking lot, noting we're secluded, but then, I can't concentrate on anything else at all. This girl is amazing, and I really want to kiss her while she strokes my cock, but I also don't want to interfere.

"Oh... God... Harper..." I moan, my head arching back against the headrest.

"Come on, baby. Give it to me," she murmurs, sliding her hand faster and harder up and down my shaft.

I grab the tissue from the console just in time to keep my pants and her dress from getting cum-stained. "Fuuuuuck."

She releases my dick. "There. Problem solved."

I'm still panting and seeing sparks at the edge of my vision. "Holy fuck."

"Ready to go in now?" she asks.

I swallow hard. "Just give me a minute. Some sexy lady just had her hand on my dick."

"Wonder who that could have been?" She grins.

Once I'm calm and have put myself back together, we're able to trickle in with the last of the guests into the Wexford.

"There you are!" Janet pounces on us the minute we're inside. "I've been wanting to do the bouquet toss."

"Before dinner?" I ask, confused.

"The caterer went to the wrong venue, so we're making it up as we go until they get here," Janet confides.

"Oh. Sorry to hear that," I reply.

Janet shrugs. "Weddings, am I right?" She waves Harper over to the gaggle of other women waiting for the bouquet toss. "One… two…" she calls with her back turned.

I know it's a setup the second Janet yells, "THREE!" and the women all part to the sides. Except a very confused Harper who is left holding the bouquet.

"Oh, how wonderful!" Janet squeals as though this is a surprise. "Now, if *only* Scott could catch the garter."

I sigh inwardly as Conner, Janet's husband, winks at me. I'm definitely going to be catching the garter, whether I want to or not. But then, everyone thinks Harper and I have been dating for a few months. They think this is a cute way to get us 'thinking about the future.'

Before I know it, garter banded around my arm, I'm dancing with Harper, the bouquet clutched between our joined hands.

"I thought the bride and groom were supposed to have the first dance," Harper whispers to me as "Love Me Tender" plays over the DJ's loudspeakers.

"Janet is nothing if not unconventional and a hopeless romantic," I reply. Tired of the hard stems between our hands, I twirl us past a nearby table and drop the bouquet onto it. "For that matter, they may have danced before we even came inside."

"That's true." She gives me a nefarious grin. Then, to my surprise, Harper lays her head on my shoulder. "Thanks for putting the flowers down. That thing was getting uncomfortable."

"I'd hate for you to be uncomfortable." I smile down at her. "Though, I do have a question."

She looks up. "What question?"

"How would you feel about staying at my place tonight?" I ask. Or rather blurt. I grimace. *Smooth, Scott. Real smooth.*

Harper regards me with an unreadable expression on her face. Then she grins. "Well, I don't think either of us have sucked on it until it's 'done' yet."

I bark out a laugh. "Is that a yes?"

She goes up on her toes and presses those perfect pink lips

against mine. I gasp and press her to open, which she does. When we finally come up for air, she murmurs, "What do you think?"

24

FOUR

Until it's Done

Harper

Oh, my God! I can't believe I just said that! I stare into the mirror in the bathroom, shocked by my own boldness.

Harper Ward would never have agreed to that proposition. And with such a dirty remark!

But then, maybe ArtIsMyLife33 would?

Somebody agreed to go home with Scott and suck his dick. Or I at least implied I was going to.

The chicken in me thinks of backing out. Scott would be polite about it, I know. The part of me who hasn't been with a man in the six months since I broke up with that controlling asshole Jack? That part wants to ride that big cock I saw in the truck, right into the sunset.

I lock eyes with myself. "Who are you?" I murmur.

The door slams open, and two drunk, giggling guests come into the restroom. "Oh, my God, did you see Scott? He is still so dreamy."

"Too bad he's taken," the other says.

Neither of them notice me, and I decide to keep it that way by slipping into a bathroom stall.

"Jessie says he is so good in bed. She says she's never had anything like it before or since," the first girl titters.

"Isn't Jessie married?" the second girl asks.

"Yeah, she is now, but that doesn't always mean it's with your best lay." The first girl is completely matter-of-fact about this. "She says his dick is huge, and he knows what to do with it."

The second girl gasps. "Married women shouldn't talk like that!"

"Pfft. Whatever. Women talk, Brianna. I mean, how else are we supposed to find the best dick?" the first woman scoffs.

"True. But Callie, if Jessie's husband ever caught her talking like that…"

"It'd be a real shit day for Jessie. Oh! Maybe we should tell him what she said! That would be funny."

I don't think it will be funny at all. I shake my head in disapproval, not that they can see it. With friends like these, does Jessie really need enemies? I don't even know the girl, and I feel sorry for her.

"Callie, that would be really bitchy, and you know it. You're not *that* drunk," Brianna says.

I can see Callie pouting as I peek through the door. She's reapplying her lipstick. "Fine, fine. I'll just see if I can't get into Scott's pants instead."

"His girlfriend has been gone for, like, fifteen minutes. I don't think that's long enough for him to lose interest." Brianna sighs at her friend.

"We'll see. Where do you think she went anyway?" Callie asks.

I decide enough is enough. It's one thing to talk about Scott's prowess in bed, but no catty young brat is creeping up on my man, rented date or not. I push open the stall door and step out. "Hi," I say cheerfully to the two women. "You must be Callie and Brianna? Nice to meet you." I wash my hands since they probably assume I was peeing.

Callie gapes at me like a caught fish. Brianna bites her lip, her shoulders shaking with suppressed laughter. "Nice to meet you too… Harper, is it?" Brianna extends her hand to me.

"That's right," I confirm. "And I thought maybe I'd go tell Jessie what a great friend Callie is. It's not every day you find someone with morals so low you can walk on them."

"Wh-what?!" Callie screeches.

"Morals. M-O-R-A-L-S. It's a set of rules a person lives by that make them a better person," I say slowly to her as though she's dumb. After what I've heard, she just might be slow on the uptake.

"You-y-you—!" Callie stutters.

Brianna puts an arm around her shoulders. Callie's only reapplied half of her dark lipstick, and it shows. "I think you need to play with somebody more on your level," Brianna says to Callie. "And give up on Scott."

Callie raises her chin and flounces through the bathroom door with Brianna in her wake.

I wonder what Brianna is doing being friends with that cow, but it's really not my business. I go back to looking at this new, bold me in the mirror.

"Yippee ki-yay, Farmer Scott." I finally grin and go back out.

I find Scott standing near the punch bowl. He's scolding two teenage boys and holding a flask above their heads.

"Wouldn't be a wedding if someone didn't try to spike the punch." I smile at Scott.

"Yeah, well, these two little hellions aren't getting away with it today," he responds, frowning at his younger family members.

I step close to Scott and slide my hand over his chest and under the lapel of his jacket. "Have you made enough of an appearance? Because I want to see this organic farm of yours."

The teenage boys smirk at each other.

Scott takes a swig, then hands them back the flask. "Have fun, boys. I'll see you later." He steers me over to Janet and Conner. "We're heading out. Congratulations again!"

"Out? But we haven't cut the cake yet!" Janet protests.

Conner clears his throat. "I think the romantic atmosphere might have convinced Harper she needs to go take a look at Scott's… works of art."

I blush. Scott grins.

"Works of art? What are you talking about. Scott doesn't have any—oh!" Janet nods vigorously. "Yes, you should go."

"Thanks for understanding." Scott and I hug them both then head out to the truck.

The drive to his farm is blessedly short. I take off McKenzy's shoes right as we get in the house. Scott shrugs out of his jacket and drapes it over a chair. Then, we crash into each other's arms, all hands and lips.

He pulls down the zipper at the back of my dress and peels it away. I fumble with the buttons on his shirt and finally get it open. The expanse of his muscular chest, sculpted by hard work, greets me, and I almost salivate.

I'm not wearing a bra so when my dress drops, my nipples harden, and Scott groans, dropping my dress to the floor, leaving me in white, lace panties and nothing else.

As he leans down to take my nipple between his lips, I know we're not going to make it to the bedroom, and I don't care. I unzip his pants and shove them down, along with his boxers, desire pulsing through me from where Scott's lips and teeth are teasing me.

He lets his shirt drop from his arms and steps out of his pants and boxers. Now all our clothes are lying in a mess on the floor.

"On the couch," he demands against my skin.

More than happy to comply, I lie down on his leather couch. The fabric is cool and sticks to my heated skin.

Scott pulls my panties off in one swift movement, tossing them aside. "Not like that," he says. "Like this."

He sits me upright and pulls my hips to the edge of the cushion, spreading my knees before him as he drops to his knees. I realize what he's going to do just before it happens, and my eyes go wide with shock.

"You're actually going to—"

"I've gotta suck on it until it's done," he replies, his blue eyes molten with lust.

"Oh, Jesus," I whisper as Scott's head descends between my thighs. The first brush of his tongue is like a lightning strike to my body. He sucks on my clit, occasionally pushing his tongue inside me and swirling it in a way that makes me see stars.

With my fingers tangled in his hair, I come hard against his mouth. Scott licks up my seam, tasting my pleasure.

He sits back on his heels, and I can see his cock standing straight and proud. There's a little pearl of cum at the tip.

"Want me to return the favor?" I pant, licking my lips and wondering what he's going to taste like.

"Yeah. I do. But I want to be inside you more," he replies. "Fuck. Condoms are in the bedroom…"

"If you're clean, I have an IUD, so…" I say, my legs still splayed wide for his viewing pleasure.

Scott draws a sharp breath. "Oh, thank God." He tugs on my hips so I slide off the couch and into his lap.

I flick my finger over the tip of his cock and taste for myself what I'm missing out on today. "Next time?" I ask coyly.

"You'd better fucking believe it," he responds, his eyes wide as he watches me taste him.

I hang onto his shoulders while he lines himself up, then sink down on his big, thick dick. I throw my head back, crying out. I've never had a dick this big.

"You okay?" he asks, his hands firm on my hips.

I nod vigorously. "Better than okay," I wheeze. He's so big, I have to ease him in gently.

He pushes up into me while pulling down on my hips, and goes even deeper. I dig my nails into his shoulders and start to move, riding him hard and fast.

We both climax at the same time, Scott's warm cum shooting up inside me while my inner muscles clamp around his cock, milking it for every drop he can give me. We collapse in a heap, much like our clothes. Sweat pours off us as we pant and lightly caress each other, coming down together.

"Scott…" I pout after a while. "I still haven't seen your works of art."

He bursts out laughing. "Oh, yes you have, baby. That was the closest thing I have to a Van Gough. Now, let me show you my Monet."

And we go for a second round.

* * *

SCOTT

Harper's phone blinks. We're lying under a blanket on the carpet next to the couch. She's asleep.

I see it's McKenzy with a whole lot of worried emojis. I'm not even sure she put actual words in there.

The screen goes black. Then lights up again with more emojis.

I nudge Harper. "I think your friend McKenzy thinks I'm an ax murderer."

"Hmm?" She looks around blearily then spots her phone half under the couch. "Oh, shit. McKenzy!" She snatches her phone from under the couch and unlocks it with a swipe of her finger.

As she texts frantically back to her friend, I twirl a lock of Harper's hair around my fingertips. It's even softer than it looks.

"McKenzy was about to call the cops," Harper groans, sliding her phone aside.

"Should I take you home?" I ask.

She raises an eyebrow at me, and I quickly amend, "I mean, only if you want me to. You can stay the night if you want to, and I really want to see you again. I owe you dinner, remember? You knocked it out of the park."

Harper smiles and sits up. "I suppose McKenzy would feel better if she actually saw me. I made sort of made a promise to help clean the apartment tomorrow."

"That sounds like more fun than a person has a right to." I chuckle and sit up too. "I want to watch you get dressed."

She laughs. "All right. You tell me where you threw my panties, and I'll get the show going."

"Oh, no," I reply. "I'm keeping those."

Her jaw drops. "You're keeping my panties?"

"Just like any good Mississippi River Slasher would," I tell her.

"Taking trophies already?"

I laugh and find her panties, handing them over to her. She takes them on and shakes her head.

I watch as she shimmies slowly into the lacy fabric. "Yep," I observe. "I can definitely die happy now."

Harper just as sexily slips back into her dress. She turns and bats her lashes at me. "Zip me up?"

I stand and put on my boxers before I zip up Harper's dress. Her smile when she turns to look at me makes my heart skip a beat.

Shit. I'm in so much trouble.

FIVE

Double Trouble

Harper

"You *slept* with him?!" McKenzy's jaw goes slack. It's the next morning, and we've finally gotten a chance to talk. When I got home the night before, I took a shower and crashed. Hard.

"Announce it to the whole apartment complex, why don't you?" I hiss. "And yes. I slept with him. It was amazing."

"Amazing? It says on the website you don't have to do the whole escort thing!" she says. "Did we forget the website?"

I snort. "I didn't do it because I thought I had to. I wanted to. We really hit it off."

"I'll say. You slept with him on the first date. And it wasn't even a proper date!" She all but wails.

"Dramatic much? You've done it before," I remind her.

"Yeah, but you're not me." McKenzy paces around me, looking me up and down. She pinches my arm.

"Hey!" I gripe.

She nods. "Okay, so I'm not dreaming."

"You're supposed to pinch yourself!" I pinch her back.

"Ouch! Fine, fine, okay. We can be super sluts together then.

But honestly, Harper, you need to stop copying me. I'm sure your parents would agree, I'm a bad influence." She grins.

My parents. "Oh, fuck."

"I mean, I wasn't going to tell them or anything. Calm down." McKenzy rubs my back as I sink into a chair. "They can't still think you're a virgin or anything like that."

I look up at her.

She blinks. "Okay, so maybe they can."

"They're very religious," I remind her. "If they knew I'd *kissed* a man on the first date, they'd lose their shit."

"We'll just say you held hands, if they ask—"

My phone dings the particular sound the At a Loose End app makes.

We both look at it. "You did give him your phone number, right?" McKenzy asks.

"Yeah, I did." I unlock my phone and stare at the screen. "It's another date."

"Well, yeah, if he wants another date, he doesn't have to buy it. You're not a sugar baby."

"It's not him. It's someone named Damien," I reply, scrolling through the request. "He needs a date for an art gallery opening tonight."

"That's short notice." McKenzy leans over me, sounding affronted on my behalf.

"It is," I agree. I hover my finger over the 'Reject' button.

She grabs my wrist. "What are you doing?"

"I'm rejecting the request. I mean, I'm dating Scott now. I should probably take my whole profile down, actually," I muse.

"So, Scott's going to pay your rent now?" she asks.

I frown. "What do you mean? Of course not!"

"That still leaves you with the money problem, honey," McKenzy points out. "If you're not getting it from Scott, where's it going to come from if not another date?"

Oh. Fuck.

"But what's Scott going to think?"

"Did he ask you not to take any more dates?" She folds her arms under her chest.

I rub the back of my neck. "No. But I thought he'd assume…"

"Better to beg forgiveness than ask permission. Besides, look at what this Damien guy is offering for the late notice. Get on it, girl!" McKenzy encourages me.

"I'll message him," I say after a beat. "If it all seems fine, then maybe, *maybe* I'll accept the date."

She grins. "There's the spirit!"

"I said maybe," I remind her.

"Yeah, yeah, get to your messaging." She waves a hand.

I go to my message center and start typing.

ArtIsMyLife33: Hi! I'm Harper. I see you sent me a date request.

Damien4: Yes. Is there a problem?

Ah. Right to the point then.

ArtIsMyLife33: No, no problem! It's just short notice and I like to feel a guy out before I go on a date with him. You know, ax murders, stranglers, kidnappers…

Damien4: I am none of those things. Every client on this site is vetted. I don't mean to be rude, but I'm very busy. You can accept the date or reject the date and I'll find someone else.

I look at the zeros after Damien's offer and ponder the brusqueness of his response. My jaw hits the floor. This guy is loaded. *Well, it's not like I'll be physically attracted to him. I may as well make some cash.*

ArtIsMyLife33: I'll take the date.

Damien4: Good. I'll see you at 7:00 PM. Please text me your address so I know where to pick you up.

I hesitate. Do I want any of these guys to have my home address? We do have good security at my building, so I send it to him.

The message is received, and then Damien signs off, abruptly cutting off our communication.

"Okay…" I mumble. I go up to my profile and accept the date.

"There, see? That's this month's rent *and* groceries taken care of!" McKenzy crows.

I jump. I'd forgotten she was here. She didn't see how much money it was, so she has no idea—it's a lot more than one month's rent.

She laughs. "Now we just need to find you something to wear. A gallery opening? How fun!"

"Right. A dress, I'm sure." I Google the gallery and realize I have absolutely nothing to wear and McKenzy doesn't either. This gallery is far too high-end for any dress that comes off the rack. Any rack.

"I'm screwed." I groan, thinking of just how much money it's going to take to get a decent-looking dress. It'll be more than Scott paid me, for sure, and that's all I have in my account at the moment.

My cell rings. I look down and see it's the front office.

"Hello?"

"Hello, Harper. This is Trish in the office. We just received a couriered package for you. The courier said it was urgent," Trish tells me.

I look at McKenzy, who shrugs, just as bewildered as I am. "Okay. I'll be right down."

McKenzy joins me as I go downstairs. "Gotta see what this is!" she remarks.

When we arrive in the office, Trish is holding out a big, flat, white box. "This just came for you," she repeats as though she didn't just tell me over the phone.

"Thanks," I say, taking the box.

"Let's go find out what it is!" McKenzy whispers excitedly.

We go back up to the apartment, set the box on the table, and I take off the lid.

There, nestled among soft tissue paper, is a gorgeous red dress.

"Holy shit," I mumble while McKenzy pulls the dress out.

"Oh, my God, where did this come from?" she asks, holding it in front of herself. "It looks like it's just your size too!" She dangles it in front of my body, looking at it critically.

I see a flat card at the bottom of the box and pick it up. In bold handwriting, it reads:

Miss Ward,
I knew you would need appropriate attire for tonight.
Please forgive my intrusiveness in procuring your address.
Sincerely,
Damien Blackwood.

McKenzy chokes on her tongue. "D-Damien *Blackwood?!*"

"What?" I ask. "Who's that?" I'm still trying to decide if I'm touched or creeped out by his gesture.

"Only one of the richest men in the United States!" she shouts.

I suddenly feel my stomach drop out. "Excuse me?"

"Ugh, Harper, you are so out of touch! Blackwood Enterprises? They just bought a chain of banks for like a couple billion dollars?" McKenzy takes my hands and starts dancing in a circle. "Girl, you have finally arrived!"

"But I really like Scott," I remind her.

"Screw Scott! He's a little fish in a little pond. Honey, you need to land this whale! All your troubles will be over," she says gleefully.

I pull my hands away. "McKenzy, I don't care that much about money. I'm not going to get myself a sugar daddy to pay my rent."

"You *need* a sugar daddy to pay your rent," she sniffs. "By the way, when he buys you a penthouse, you remember the little people like your best friend McKenzy, right?"

I roll my eyes. "It's one dress and one date. What's the most that could happen?"

"Just keep your options open, that's all I'm saying." She smiles mischievously.

Shaking my head, I take the dress into my bedroom and slip it on. It fits perfectly. *Was he searching dates by their measurements so he could have the girl fit the dress? Whatever. It doesn't matter.* I put on my best jewelry, Grandma Ward's diamond earrings and matching pendant, then realize I still don't have proper shoes.

I swing my door open to find McKenzy standing there, holding the perfect pair of Stewart Weitzmans. "Thank God you're a shoe junkie."

"I know. You love me for it." She sets them on the concrete

floor, and I slip them on. "And thank God we're the same shoe size."

"Agreed," I reply.

"Okay, do the little twirl. I know you want to." McKenzy grins at me.

Despite my nervousness over the date with one of the richest men in the country, I have to laugh. I turn in a circle for her. She primps and fluffs and finally stands back, satisfied.

"Go get 'em, girl!" she says.

"It's just a date!" I reiterate. I glance at my phone. "And I've got hours. I'm going to go change and catch up on some artwork."

"All right, but when it's time to go, you're going to knock him dead!"

I roll my eyes and go back to my room to take the dress off before I ruin it. I lay everything out for later and then get to work. I'm lost in my artwork when my phone dings. I look down, hoping it's Scott.

It's not. It's from an unknown number.

"Forgive the intrusion, but I wanted to let you know I'll be there to pick you up in thirty minutes."

Oh, fuck! What time is it? I barely shoot off an answer that I'll be ready and then rush to get back in the dress and fix my makeup. Smokey eyes are never easy!

My phone dings again. "I'm downstairs and hoping you're ready early. I like to get to these things on time."

Fashionably late. Right. I add his number to my contacts.

Harper Ward: As a matter of fact, I am ready. I will be right down."

Damien Blackwood: Excellent, thank you.

I turn to McKenzy. "He's here."

"What? He texted you? How the fuck did he get your number?!" she gapes.

"I don't know. Rich guy access?" I speculate.

"Huh. Okay, don't let him do anything weird to you," she says, suddenly suspicious.

"Oh, so what happened to 'landing the whale'?" I ask cheekily.

"That was before I knew he had a stalking fetish," McKenzy grumbles. "Be safe. Text me before he goes all Christian Grey."

I dump what I need from my silver clutch into my black one. "Yeah, right. Honestly, McKenzy, it's just one date and it's for pay. I don't see myself ending up in a playroom with a ball gag in my mouth."

"Uh-huh." She looks skeptical but still shoves me out the door. "Good luck!"

"I'm not going to need luck," I scoff, heading to the elevator. No way I'm taking the stairs in these shoes.

I walk out the front door and stop in my tracks. There's a stretch limo with an honest-to-God uniformed driver, hat and all, holding the door to the back seat open.

"Holy shit," I whisper under my breath.

I start toward the limo, but instead of me just sliding inside, Damien Blackwood himself steps out. He looks a bit grumpy for a moment, like that's his usual disposition. Then his frown fades, and he gives me a smile. "Miss Ward," he greets me in a deep, velvety voice.

My jaw is on the sidewalk. I have to remind myself to close my mouth. Damien Blackwood is *hot*. Tall, dark, and handsome hot.

"Uh, H-Harper, Mr. Blackwood. Harper's just fine," I manage. His green eyes are sharp, intelligent and hungry. He has the eyes of predator—or a man who has the skills to make billions in the boardroom.

"Damien, please," he responds. He takes my hand and kisses the back of it. "You're even more breathtaking in person."

My knees go weak when his lips brush against my skin. "Thanks," I murmur. "You aren't so bad yourself."

Damien gestures to the open limo door and helps me inside. "We're ready to go, Frederick," he tells the driver once he's settled in beside me.

He smells like some undefinable high-end cologne. Every time I breathe it in, I want to swoon.

"I'm sorry about the late invitation and contacting you directly by phone. I was able to locate your number through my… associates," Damien says, though he doesn't sound sorry at all.

I know I'm not. "That's okay. I was having a dress dilemma right when you sent the package anyway."

"I confess, I was going to send that dress to a young woman I was dating, but we had a rather messy break-up last night. I looked you up by your measurements," Damien confirms. He looks me up and down and my skin positively sizzles. "You wear it better than she could."

"Thanks," I reply awkwardly. We pass a tan sedan I think I recognize, but I'm too flustered to give it much thought.

"And that's the last I'm going to say about any other woman tonight." Damien smirks. He rests his hand on mine on the seat between us.

I swallow. *Lord, am I in trouble!*

SIX

Mr. Billionaire

Damien

What an unexpected pleasure. I watch Harper's cheeks flush as our shoulders touch in the limo. Honestly, I should be sitting further away from her. There's plenty of seating in the limo's expansive back section after all. But since I first laid eyes on her, I've been utterly captivated.

Today, I just wanted someone who checked all the right boxes for the dress. Tonight, I'm realizing I might have found someone who checks all the right boxes for me.

"Have you been to an art gallery opening before?" I ask conversationally, my hand still boldly laid over hers. I'm not a man who lets what he wants get away.

She swallows, and it draws my attention to the elegant lines of her neck. "No, Damien. I haven't."

"I think you'll find it rather entertaining," I continue. "Especially given your art background. Or am I making too many assumptions about your username? Are you an art history major?"

Harper pauses, then admits, "I'm an artist. Mostly a painter."

Intriguing. "Really? Then again, I suppose given the criteria for living at Carleton Artist Lofts, you must dabble in something."

Her sea green eyes flash and I know I've hit a nerve, but then, I was trying to. I hide my smile and wait for her to put me in my place.

"Actually, I don't 'dabble.' It's my career." She is now glaring at me. Ah, the passion in that glare!

I feel my cock twitch. I feign surprise. "Oh. I didn't know. Have you sold much?"

That's a sharp blow, I can tell, and her shoulders slump–with mutiny, not defeat. "Not yet."

"Pity. I'm sure your work is lovely." I smile.

She looks me up and down, her eyes narrowed. "You're winding me up on purpose."

Now I'm really surprised. "Huh. I'll be damned. Most of the women I associate with don't catch on this quickly."

"Most of the women you associate with are probably idiots," she mutters.

I throw my head back and laugh. "I can't argue with you there. But, you know, alliances with wealthy families whose daughters haven't had to do jack shit but get mani-pedis and swim around in their pools don't always make it as interesting for me."

"Then I'd suggest you stop trying to ally yourself with wealthy families' daughters before your heir comes out with an IQ of two," Harper replies.

I grimace. "I am in no hurry to have an heir, trust me."

"Aren't you graying at the temples?" she needles me. "Maybe you should get on that."

It's all right. I know just how to get her back. "Are you volunteering?"

Her eyes widen. Her jaw goes slack. "What?"

* * *

HARPER

I think I'm dying of shock, but I'm not sure if I'm having heart palpitations because I'm horrified—or interested! Which, in turn, horrifies me even more.

I'm not that desperate for money—am I? I shriek in my head. But then, I know it has nothing to do with money. I'm sure any woman with a pulse given that offer would climb him like he's a jungle gym just because of how handsome he is. He's also well-spoken and confident.

I remember what he said about my art and fold my arms over my peaked nipples. *Down girl.*

"I'm joking," Damien laughs. He boops me on the nose, and I want to bite his finger off. "I just wanted to see what you would do."

"You like pushing people's buttons, don't you?" I say flatly. It's not a question.

Damien winks at me. "It's what I do for a living, and it's immensely entertaining. You don't seem so bad at it yourself. Maybe you should come work for me."

"I already have a job I love, thanks," I reply.

"Starving artist?" he teases.

I purse my lips. "I'm not starving."

"Right. Because a woman like you likes 'long walks on the beach' and 'a good party,'" he quotes.

I groan, dropping my head into my hands. "I really need to edit my profile."

"Did Miss McKenzy Jasper come up with that?" he guesses. Correctly.

"Did you hire a stalker or do the work yourself?" I ask, exasperated.

He chuckles. "The Internet is a wonderful invention."

"So, you do your own stalking. Good to know," I add.

We pull up to the venue I'd seen online, and I watch women in dazzling dresses step out of limousines, town cars, and other vehicles more expensive than a house on Lake Minnetonka. They swish down a red carpet, photographers crowded on either side, taking pictures of them and their dashing partners all wearing Armani or something similar.

"I'm going to be on the cover of *Time*, aren't I, showing up with you?" I gasp, feeling sick to my stomach.

"Probably the entertainment section of the *Star Tribune*. I'm not that much of a celebrity," Damien chuckles.

Fuck. What about Scott? What if he sees this?

Then again, McKenzy did point out that he's not paying my rent, and he never asked me not to go on any other dates.

I'm not going to know any of these people. They're going to think I'm some worthless outsider.

"On my arm, you are just another bauble. No one will even notice you," Damien reassures me.

That should have been insulting, but strangely, it makes me feel better. *I am a Rolex watch.*

I square my shoulders. "Okay, let's do this."

Damien grins, and then it's our turn on the red carpet. Frederick, our chauffeur, strides confidently around the limo to open the door and let us out. My date gets out first, then holds out his hand to me.

I take a deep breath. *I am just a Rolex watch* and take his hand.

The second I step out of the limo, people start snapping pictures. Film cameras point in our direction, and reporters start shouting.

"Mr. Blackwood! Mr. Blackwood! Who are you escorting tonight?" is the gist of the shouting, a cacophony of voices overlapping and fighting to one-up each other.

I suppress a glare and force a smile instead, waving to the crowd. "Just a bauble?" I hiss out the side of my mouth.

Damien's shoulders shake with suppressed mirth. "I may have under-exaggerated," he whispers back, tucking my hand into his arm. To the crowd, he smiles widely and says, "This is Miss Harper Ward, an artist in her own right. I am honored she agreed to pause her very busy schedule to spend an evening with me."

I look up at him, all the blood in my head draining to my toes. *Oh, my. Did he just...*

I'm going to have to call the teensy, weensy little coffee shop selling my work and give them a heads up. Lord only knows if his words will stick, but for now, I've got some buzz and The Witch's Brew needs to be warned about paparazzi about to descend.

The reporters mumble amongst themselves, searching for me on their phones as we walk through the door and into the gallery itself.

"Did… did you just…?" I gawk at him. "You haven't even seen my work!"

"I don't have to. Only a fool pursues something with the kind of passion and dedication you do who isn't any good at it, and you're no fool. Though, if you'd like to show me some of your art sometime, I'd be delighted." Damien smiles.

"I'd… I'd love to," I find myself responding.

His eyes crinkle at the corner in a real, genuine smile this time. "Good." We walk into the gallery, but at first, I can barely pull my eyes away from him. I blink a few times to clear my mind.

Finally, I manage to look past him and see a Michael Vernon. A lot of Michael Vernons.

While I'd assumed he'd be featured at the gallery opening tonight, I am shocked to see his work has taken up every gallery wall.

I have to stop myself from squealing and jumping around like a fangirl.

"So, this Michael Vernon, is he any good?" Damien asks.

My head snaps back around. "Are you…serious?"

He shrugs. "I'm not really an art aficionado. I generally depend on others to do my decorating at the office and at home. I'd like to know if it's worth getting one of his paintings."

I make a sound like air escaping a balloon. "You need me to tell you that *Michael Vernon* is a good artist?"

"Yes," he replies, no teasing in his tone this time. "You're a sharp young woman. I value your opinion."

"He's… Damien, he's my favorite!" I gush, gesturing at the nearest painting. "Do you see his bold use of color and how the layering of the paint also reflects how weighted down the subject is? He finds beauty in the most ordinary, everyday people and can tell their whole life stories with one stroke of his brush! If I had the talent he has in one of his pinkies, I'd be over the moon!"

"Ah, Damien, you finally found one with some art sense," a portly older man with a strategic combover, but a very nice suit, chortles as he turns to us. He has a white scarf draped over his shoulders in the universal I-*am*-an-art-aficionado look.

"Please, Julian. You know as well as I do that this is the first time I've shown up anywhere with a woman with any sense at all." Damien gives me another of his eye-crinkling smiles. "I rather like it."

I can feel my cheeks heating up.

"Tell me, young lady, what is it you do for a living?" Julian asks me. "I know you can't possibly work for this stuffy old fart."

"Old fart! I'm forty-five, you pompous ass!" Damien banters back.

"You forgot to add 'fat' this time. You must really like this one." Julian's eyes reflect his good humor. "I really am curious."

I fidget with my clutch. "I'm… um… an artist, sir. A painter."

Julian's eyes light up. "Really? How exciting. And at the beginning of your career, no doubt. Damien always snaps up good potential before anyone else can, the bastard. And it's not 'sir.' Please, call me Julian." He extends his hand.

I clasp it, and he brings it to his lips. "Harper," I respond. "Very nice to meet you."

"Harper. What a lovely name." Julian releases my hand.

"Harper is going to show me her work," Damien states proudly.

Julian snorts. "What, you want to go over to her place to see her paintings? Come now, my dear Harper, don't fall for that. I'm sure you have some pictures on your phone."

Embarrassed, I still dutifully pull out my phone and scroll through my photos to a couple of examples of my artwork.

Julian draws a sharp breath and snatches my phone from me. "Why, these are exquisite! Damien, since when do *you* have any taste?! I must have this one for my villa in Toledo."

"That's in Spain," Damien clarifies, in case I might think he means Ohio.

"How wonderful." I smile at Julian. "I minored in Spanish."

Damien looks intrigued. "Well, well, so many layers. Like your friend Michael Vernon's paintings."

"Friend? I wish…" I sigh.

"Oh, why of course, Harper. How remiss of me. Michael? Michael, over here!" Julian calls, waving to a man in a leather jacket, black boots, ripped jeans, and a T-shirt. When he turns around, I see it reads 'Meh.'

But then I lift my eyes and see that Michael Vernon is walking toward us.

I think I may hyperventilate. The god of my world, gray-haired but still hanging onto his biker boy charm, is now standing in my presence.

"Michael, this is Harper," Julian says, gesturing to me. "She's an artist—a good one. Look." He hands *the* Michael Vernon my phone.

He examines it, blowing up pictures with his fingers, tilting his head this way and that. "A young Picasso couldn't ask for a better start." He nods and hands my phone back to Julian, who hands it back to me.

I swear I'm going to faint. Or burst into tears. "Th-thank you, sir," I whisper.

"Please, call me Michael. We're colleagues in the same profession after all, Harper," he says.

"Yes. Yes, of course. Thank you, Michael." I manage to sound professional. I think. At least I didn't squeak like a little mouse. *Michael Vernon likes my work!* My brain throws a party, complete with confetti poppers and fireworks.

If I die right now, I'll die happy. And it's all because of Damien.

SEVEN

A Better Start

Harper

The rest of the evening is a blur. Michael has to circulate, of course, but he comes back to Damien and me frequently to check in. He asks where I'm showing my work. I blush and say, "The Witch's Brew coffee shop on Lake Street in Minneapolis."

Michael grins at me. "A perfect place to start."

"You'll have to give some pieces to a proper gallery now, though. People will be wondering where to find your work," Damien whispers in my ear.

"Because you announced it in front of the press!" I reply.

Damien gives me an innocent look. "Did I do that?"

I squeeze his arm in gratitude, and he laughs.

It's late by the time we leave Michael, Julian and the rest of Damien's acquaintances at the gallery. I can't help but note that Damien didn't call any of them his friends.

"Do your friends not attend gallery openings?" I ask.

Damien winces at me. "Caught that, did you? I don't have a lot of friends, Harper. A man like me makes a lot of enemies. I do have one good friend, Laurence Killian, but he's in New York. My main business is in the Big Apple, so I spend most of my time there. I do keep a penthouse in Minneapolis, though. I've been doing a fair amount of business here recently. So, I'll probably be in the market for another date not long from now."

"What, like pay me? You've got to be joking. You hooked me up with Michael Vernon! If I had it to give, you could have a kidney, my liver, and my virginity!" I respond.

Damien raises an eyebrow, and I blush, looking away. Sometimes my mouth moves faster than my brain.

A tan sedan with its windows down peels away from the curb just as Frederick comes around the limo to open the back door. It nearly hits the poor chauffeur, and he shakes his fist at the other driver, unleashing a litany of curse words.

The driver then turns to us. Damien has an eyebrow raised. "Sorry," Frederick says contritely, his cheeks flushing.

"I don't think I've ever heard so many eloquent conjugations of the word 'fuck.'" Damien chuckles, clapping Frederick on the back.

The driver relaxes and resumes his professional persona, opening the back door of the limo for us. "Shall we go back to the penthouse, Mr. Blackwood?" he asks.

Damien looks at me, his eyes dark with desire. "I don't know," he purrs. "Shall we go back to the penthouse, Miss Ward?"

I know if I say 'no,' he won't feel slighted or refuse another date with me, and he isn't going to want me to say 'yes' out of some perceived obligation after he introduced me to Michael Vernon. But… after this delightful evening of one-upping each other and educating him about art while he listened with genuine interest, I want to. I want to say 'yes.'

So I do.

"Yes, let's go back to the penthouse, Mr. Blackwood."

It's not as though Scott and I are exclusive, after all. We've only had one date.

Damien smiles at me like a wolf smiles at a lamb and helps me into the limo. "Honestly, I wasn't expecting you to say yes."

"I know," I reply. "But I'm curious to see what your decorator calls 'art.'"

He throws his head back and laughs. "Is that all, little red bird?"

Little red bird. I kind of like that. "Well, I mean, I'm sure there are a few pieces in your bedroom."

"That there are, and I can't wait to show you the biggest piece of all."

* * *

DAMIEN

How very unexpected… and delightful. This freckle-nosed goddess is going to ride my dick tonight.

I'm practically salivating. I hope she doesn't want the grand tour of all the art in the penthouse. I don't think I can be patient that long.

I subtly watch the rise and fall of her chest as I extend my arm behind her along the seat of the limo. I want to take her right here, right now. But that would be both cliché and undignified, and I am neither of those things.

As the limo crawls toward my penthouse in downtown Minneapolis, I play with some stray waves of Harper's hair. She must use a lilac shampoo, body wash, or lotion. Whichever it is, I'm looking forward to burying my nose in it.

Finally, we arrive at the underground parking ramp. Frederick comes around the limo, and I try not to spring out like my dick wants to from my pants. I am not some young schoolboy after all. I can be patient. Suave. Seductive.

Harper takes my hand and steps out of the limousine, looking around at the concrete pillars and other vehicles around us. "Is this a Banksy?" she teases me.

"A what?" I ask.

She shakes her head. "He's a street artist."

"Oh, got it. Ha ha." I'm not familiar, but I like her sarcastic attitude and quick wit. I take out my fob that will tell the elevator to go straight up to the penthouse. "Come with me."

She's a bit nervous now.

Cute.

I squeeze her hand. "Nothing's going to happen that you don't want. If we get upstairs and you decide you only want to look at my artwork and go home, that's just fine by me." After all, I have every intention of taking her out again. My dick might be disappointed tonight, but I certainly wouldn't be. Just being in the company of this fascinating woman is enough to make my night.

"Okay." Her smile is still a little nervous, but she also looks relieved.

Art tour it is. I tug Harper along with me to the elevator, and it takes us up to the top floor. "You might also like the view," I tell her nonchalantly as the elevator doors open to my living room with its long bank of floor-to-ceiling windows on the other side.

She gasps and walks over to the windows. "Holy shit! This view is amazing!"

"I know." I smile and slip my arm around her waist as I join her at the windows. "Perhaps you will paint it sometime."

"That would be fabulous!" she gushes. Then her cheeks flush. "I mean, if it's okay for me to come back."

"I'll have management make you a fob," I say. I wasn't planning to; I barely know her after all. But being here with her now makes me want to give her the keys to everything I own. The mansion in Connecticut. The jet. The corporate building. My safety-deposit box with its two million in cash. Whatever her little heart desires.

This isn't like me at all. I'm not the kind of guy to fall hard for a woman. Fuck, I'm not the kind of guy to fall for a woman at all. But Harper's different. She's intelligent. She's a hard worker, and she's motivated. I like all of those things about her. The more time I spend with her, the more I want to give her everything she could ever desire.

Her dazzling smile makes my heart thump, and it's more than enough reward for my gesture. "Really? You'd do that for me?"

"I find I might do just about anything for you, my little red bird," I whisper, more honestly than I intend.

Harper throws herself into my arms and hugs me. "I can't believe you're not married yet! You're so generous, kind, and thoughtful...." She frowns. "Wait, you're not married, are you? I mean, McKenzy made it sound like you were the world's most eligible bachelor, and you said you broke up with your girlfriend, but…"

"But rich guys like to keep a side piece?" I grin. "I'm divorced. Nothing to worry about, little red bird."

She sags with relief then blushes with embarrassment. "Sorry. I just wanted to make sure."

"I'm not offended. Well, not *too* offended. I think it speaks to your integrity that you're checking ahead of time." I give her a sly smile. "Are you seeing anyone? Maybe a certain Scott Bauer?"

Harper groans and presses her forehead into my chest. "Stalker."

"You like that about me. Come now, tell me the truth," I tease.

She snorts. "I don't have to tell you anything. This is just a date from an app, remember?" She has a mischievous twinkle in her eye, so I know she's teasing.

"I am twenty years your senior. I'm old enough to be your father," I point out.

"Yeah, well, I'm not into that daddy stuff, so I'll just go ahead and tell you." She gives me a sheepish smile. "I am seeing Scott, but we haven't agreed to be exclusive or anything."

I nod. "Good. I'm glad. I'm gone so often, I like that you'll have someone else to spend your time with while I'm away."

She blinks at me. "You don't mind?"

"Not one bit," I respond. I've shocked her, I can tell. And I like it. "So, are you ready for your tour?"

"Sure," she says after gathering herself. "Want to start in the bedroom?"

Why not shock her more? I slip a sleeve off her shoulder, exposing her creamy skin. "Why not start right here?" I murmur.

Then I kiss her shoulder and all the way up her neck while I subtly draw down the zipper of her dress.

* * *

HARPER

The dress pools at my feet, leaving me in McKenzy's black high-heeled Steward Weitzman's, black lace panties, and nothing else. The neck of the dress had been too wide for a bra, and its structure was such that I really hadn't needed one.

Damien draws a sharp breath, pulling his lips away from my neck to look at my exposed body. "Perfect," he whispers. "Absolutely perfect. I swear, I'm having you sculpted and placed in my foyer in the Connecticut house."

I imagine the 'Connecticut house' is actually a mansion, but these rich types have quaint little names for their dwellings, I guess. I reach for the buttons on Damien's shirt as he slips out of his jacket.

"Let me take care of that," he offers, taking my hands and kissing my fingertips. Then he moves them downward to cup his cock through his pants. "You take care of this."

I wonder why he doesn't want me messing with his shirt. But then I see him remove diamond-and-gold cufflinks with large enough stones that they could have made two very expensive engagement rings. The buttons themselves are tricky, I can tell.

"Go on. Get your hands on it." Damien grins.

I do want to 'get my hands on it.' I pull down his fly and unbutton his pants, seeing black silk boxers beneath. They must be expensive.

But I can also see he's started leaking cum, wetting the front of the boxers. *How long was he lusting after me tonight?*

With a push, his boxers and pants are on the floor. He springs free, his impressive cock pointing straight at me. I ache to have it inside me and know I'm soaking my panties. I stroke my hand over his shaft, thumbing the trickle of semen coming out of the tip.

"Turn and face the windows," Damien says, tossing his shirt aside, now naked before me.

"Giving orders now?" I shiver. I like it.

"Yes." Then he spins me around and presses me to the window. His hands reach up between me and the glass to massage my breasts, tweaking my nipples.

One hand goes lower, sliding down my belly and into my

panties. I gasp as his experienced hand slips two fingers inside my wet entrance, his thumb working my clit.

"Fuck yourself on my fingers," Damien commands me, and I do what he says, riding his hand while he finger-fucks me. "Good girl."

I come around his fingers, whimpering for more. "Please," I beg.

He withdraws his fingers and pushes my panties down until they fall around my ankles. "Please what?"

"Please, f-fuck me," I stutter wildly.

"There's my good girl." He presses the head of his cock just inside my entrance.

I want to push back on him and greedily take more inside, but his grip is vice-like on my hips, stopping me.

"Oh, god," I plead.

"Press your tits against the glass and brace yourself," he orders me. "I want anyone who's watching to get a good look."

Watching?! I look out the windows, glancing around at other windows that might just have a peeping Tom. I know the idea should scare me, or repulse me, but I feel excited for some reason.

I spread my legs wider and press my breasts against the glass, my nipples hardening at the coolness.

"That's my good girl," Damien whispers in my ear.

Then, in one powerful movement, he thrusts his whole length inside me.

EIGHT

Against the Window

Harper

I cry out, pleasure radiating through my body as Damien reaches around and thumbs my clit in time with his hard, deep thrusts.

"How does it feel, little red bird?" he asks as he makes me come again.

"S-So good." My teeth chatter, and my knees are weak.

He forces a third orgasm out of my body. Then a fourth. And still he doesn't cum.

"Damien," I beg. "Please." Damien must be close. I know he has to be close. "Please, Damien, cum inside me!"

"Mmm, my good girl." He slaps my ass, and my whole body tenses. I come again, and this time, as my body spasms around him, he finally grunts a few times and joins me.

He groans, and his whole body shudders, but he's still holding me up when my knees give out and I would have slid down the glass. He keeps pumping in and out of me until both our tremors cease.

I can't believe I just fucked a billionaire! I look back over my shoulder, and Damien is giving me a dirty look, as though he can read my mind.

"Do you always last that long?" I ask him.

Damien chuckles. "No. You're just that sexy." He slips his cock out of me. "Damn, little red bird, I haven't had it this good in years."

"I'd tell you I've never had it this good," I reply, almost wheezing. "But I don't want to over-inflate your ego."

"Oh, I know you've never had it this good. You've never been with a mature man who knows what he's doing." He grins. "Now, how about a naked art tour? I promise we'll end up in the bedroom and have more of the same. How do you like that plan?"

My whole body tingles in anticipation. "I'd like that very much."

This time, I'll be sure to text McKenzy so she doesn't worry about me.

* * *

AS DAMIEN PULLS UP in front of Carleton Artist Lofts in his black Lamborghini Sunday morning, I notice a tan sedan drive slowly by us. For a second, I think I recognize the driver, but I only see the back of his head, so I can't be sure. I shake my head. It's probably another renter I've seen in the hallways.

"I'm flying back to New York in a few hours. I'll let you know when I'm back in town," Damien says, cupping my cheek.

"Okay," I respond, giving him a wicked smile.

Damien laughs and then presses his lips to mine in a searing kiss. "Go on. I'm sure McKenzy is pacing the floor about to burst."

"Probably," I agree. I kiss him again then get out of the car. "Have a safe trip."

"Have lots of great dates, little red bird," he replies. He watches to make sure I get into the apartment building then pulls away with a wave.

As Damien predicted, McKenzy is all a-twitter and launches into a barrage of questions as soon as I walk through the door.

"Oh, my God! Oh, my God!" she all but screams. "Did you sleep with Damien Blackwood? One of the richest men in America?"

"Well, to be fair, we didn't do much sleeping..." I confess, smiling as McKenzy wraps me up in a bone-crushing hug.

"I knew it! I just *knew* you'd hit it off. Now, all your financial troubles are over!"

I frown at her. "McKenzy, I'm not going to fuck him for money."

"Why not? You need it. He has it. Win-win," she says.

"I don't want to be his sugar baby." I blush, however, thinking it wouldn't be that bad of a deal.

"Seriously? Man, you are missing a HUGE opportunity here." She sighs, shaking her head at me as though I'm out of my mind.

"Seriously," I reply firmly.

McKenzy rolls her eyes. "Ugh. You and your morals. I swear."

"Speaking of which, Damien already provided me with enough money to get me through this month and most of next," I remind her. "And I'm going to keep dating him, but not for money anymore. He's flying out to New York this afternoon, but he'll be back."

"You mean, you're not even going to take dates with him through the app anymore? Girl, how are you going to get rent money?" McKenzy demands. "You're not getting it from Scott either, so...?"

"I'll figure it out. Damien practically threw me at the feet of the art world last night. Maybe I'll get some sales or commissions or something. Who knows?" I say excitedly.

"Really?" She jumps up and down. "That's fantastic!"

My cell rings, and I pull it out of my clutch. I recognize the number to The Witch's Brew. "Hang on a sec, McKenzy. I need to get this."

"Sure, sure." She sits down in one of her chairs and watches me with interest.

When I answer, Rebecca, the owner, starts right in. "Harper! You're never going to believe this. Some guy named Julian Price just walked in here and *bought every single piece* of your art! And he paid double!"

"He paid double?" I think of Julian and feel a little bad. "He didn't have to do that."

"He said he'll probably get thousands for them, so I wouldn't feel too bad," Rebecca explains. "And then Michael Vernon, the man himself, came in here! He was disappointed that your paintings were gone, but he also said he was proud of you and you deserve it. He wanted me to give him your number. I thought that was okay."

I swear I'm going to pee myself with excitement. "That's great! No, really, thank you for giving him my number."

"He also said our coffee is to die for," Rebecca continues proudly. "Maybe we'll be the next big artist hangout, and it's all because of you! I can't thank you enough, Harper. I don't know what you did, but keep doing it! Oh, and I need more paintings. Unless you're too big time now for a little coffee shop. I'd totally understand."

"I'll never be too big for a little coffee shop," I reply, grinning from ear to ear. "I'll have to finish some pieces I've been working on, but you can expect more within a week."

"That's great! I'll see you soon." She hangs up.

McKenzy is squirreling around in her chair. "So?"

"The paintings at The Witch's Brew have completely sold out," I tell her, dazed.

"Well then, what are you waiting for? Get your ass over to that easel and finish something!" McKenzy stabs a finger in the direction of my painting corner situated under the tall loft windows. With a smile, I head over to get started on a new painting.

* * *

IT'S the Wednesday after my very full weekend. I'm just adding a touch of green to one of my canvases, and sitting back to see if it needs any more finishing touches, when my phone dings the At a Loose End tone.

"Shit," I grumble. "I forgot to take down my profile." I go in, and out of curiosity, look at who's requested me.

I do a double-take. "No fucking way!"

"What?" McKenzy asks, looking up from where she's sketching designs for a new sofa on her tablet.

"It's my ex!" I gape, setting down my brush and pallet and going over to show her my screen.

"No fucking way." She sets her tablet on the coffee table and snatches my phone from me. "Oh, my God. It really is Rafael!"

Rafael–known as 'Bullet' in the NFL–and I were high school sweethearts. McKenzy knows this. In fact, I cried on her shoulder when we broke up. That was years ago, before he made it big time.

"So, this asshole is trying to get back with you through an app? After he cheated on you with your friend?" she shouts indignantly.

"Guess so," I seethe.

"What a jackass! Here, let me reply. I'll write something that will make his balls shrivel off," she promises. "I mean, the fucking gall— holy shit!"

"What?" I ask, plopping down next to her on the couch she designed last year. Artistic, yet comfortable, McKenzy's whole life motto.

She points at the offer. "Do you *see* how much he's offering?!"

I look where she's pointing. Then my eyes just about bug out of my head. "No way."

"I didn't know you were capable of adding that many zeroes on At a Loose End!" She opens the offer and we both stare once more. "Looks like it's legit."

"Is he out of his damn mind?" I gasp.

McKenzy looks thoughtful. "Actually, I think you should take the date."

"What? Why? My art gig's picking up–"

"Yeah," she interrupts. "But it's always good to have something in reserve, and you can also tell this sleaze, to his face, what you think of him trying to buy you."

"If I go on a date with him, isn't that the same as letting him buy me?" I ask dubiously.

"Nah. This is you fleecing his dumb ass for money then telling him he can shove his head right back up his ass," she replies. "I mean, for real, he *owes* you at least this much. He slept with your friend!"

I press my lips into a thin line, starting to come around to McKenzy's way of thinking. "He did sleep with my friend," I mutter.

"See? There you go. Get some of your own back." She hands my phone back to me. "Accept."

With a defiant lift to my chin, I do. I accept.

* * *

BULLETVIKING: Hey, Harper. Never thought you'd accept my request.

I look at my screen flash Rafael's message and choose to ignore it, going back to layering some blue paint on an abstract sky.

BulletViking: I know you're still mad at me.

"No shit, Sherlock," I grunt.

BulletViking: I swear I didn't sleep with Melody. I don't even like her. Fuckin' bitch.

That made two of us, but I wasn't going to respond to him. I'd heard it straight from the horse's mouth he'd slept with my friend. She'd even provided proof!

BulletViking: I don't know how she got a pair of my boxers...

"Maybe because you left them in her room?" I reply snidely to the phone, even though he can't hear me.

BulletViking: Come on, Harper. Please talk to me. Yell at me. Scream. Call me names. Something.

I grind my teeth, then pick up the phone.

ArtIsMyLife33: Are you seriously going to try to tell me you didn't sleep with Melody?

BulletViking: I didn't! I swear I didn't!

ArtIsMyLife33: Yeah, right. I don't even know why you contacted me for a date, you masochist!

BulletViking: I don't know why you're on a pay-to-date site. Are you hard up for money, sugar?

ArtIsMyLife33: Don't you "sugar" me, you son of a bitch! If you'd offered a penny less, I'd have rejected your offer and let McKenzy shrivel your balls off!

BulletViking: LOL, shrivel my balls off? How was she going to do that?

ArtIsMyLife33: I don't know. But it would have been epic.

BulletViking: I have no doubt. I'd rather you shrivel my balls off, though.

ArtIsMyLife33: I will on Friday!

BulletViking: LOL! I'm looking forward to it.

I growl at the phone and start stabbing the off button, when a thought occurs to me.

ArtIsMyLife33: What are YOU doing on a pay-to-date site?

BulletViking: How about you ask me on Friday, sugar?

ArtIsMyLife33: I will. And don't call me "sugar"!

NINE

Sugar Baby

Harper

On Thursday, I get another ding on my phone from At a Loose End. I sigh. If it weren't for the fact I haven't been paid for my date with Damien yet, I'd have taken down my profile by now. I need that payment to process and hit my bank account!

I look at my screen. Tomás. He's offering less than anyone else I've dated for me to go with him to a quinceañera on Saturday. I know I should decline, but a message pings right away, and I feel compelled to read what he has to say.

EspanolEsVida1: I know I haven't offered a lot, but please hear me out **@ArtIsMyLife33**. My ex-wife is going to be at my niece's quinceañera this Saturday, and she's bringing a date. I absolutely, positively *have* to bring a younger, hotter date. I know that sounds shallow, but this woman destroyed my life. She destroyed *me*. She cheated, and my niece *still* wants her at her quinceañera. I'm desperate. Help!

Thinking back on what Rafe did to me, I am galvanized into action.

ArtIsMyLife33: Please, call me Harper. And I'm in. I've been cheated on before as well

EspanolEsVida1: Thank you so much for understanding. I will pick you up around 6:30 PM on Saturday. Where would you like to meet?

I think of the co-op, then decide against it. This poor man's suffered enough.

ArtIsMyLife33: I live at the Carleton Artist Lofts in St. Paul. Does that work for you?

EspanolEsVida1 Thank you for trusting me, Harper. I will be there at 6:30 PM on Saturday.

ArtIsMyLife33: Thank you for trusting me. I know it's got to be hard telling a complete stranger what happened to you. Oh, and may I call you Tomás?

EspanolEsVida1 I'd like that very much. Until Saturday.

ArtIsMyLife33: ¡Hasta luego!

I set my phone aside. All right, so it's Scott and Damien, a one-time fuck-off date with Rafe, and a favor for Tomás. I think it'll be fine. After all, there is no chance of me getting back with Rafe, and Tomás is just a paid date out of desperation.

Yes, everything is going to be fine.

I return to my canvas, starting to dab some coral hues into the skyline I'd been working on so painstakingly.

My phone rings.

I look over with a frown. *Who even calls nowadays when you can text?*

The ID flashes up and my frown turns to a scowl.

Bitch

Since I've sworn never to speak to her again, Melody must be calling because someone died or was grievously injured. I snatch up the phone. "Are your Mom and Dad okay?"

Melody giggles, and I know I've made a terrible mistake. "I know your secret."

"Really? I know yours. You're a lying, cheating C-U-N-T of a friend, and I hope you get hit by a bus. Goodbye, Melody." I start to hang up the phone.

"You're going out with Rafe on Friday," she sing-songs at me.

"And? How's that any of your business?" I can't believe I'm still engaging with her! *I should just hang up.*

I slide my thumb over the red circle on the screen, but then she says something that makes my blood freeze. "I saw you in the Entertainment section of *The Star Tribune.* Looks like you're already seeing Damien Blackwood. If you want to get back with Rafe, I'd suggest you end it with Damien. Or maybe I should just tell your parents their goody two-shoes daughter is playing the field. I guess you're a super slut now."

"Like you?" I ask harshly. But my ears are still ringing. *She'd really tell my parents I'm dating more than one guy?!*

Of course she would. This is Melody we're talking about here. I don't know what inspired my friend to hate me so much, but she does, and has, clearly, for longer than I realized since she stole my boyfriend from me in high school.

"Oh, honey, you can't juggle men like I can," Melody chuckles. "You can't even keep one man. And all you had to do was believe him!"

"What's that supposed to mean?" I respond, confused. *Disengage, Harper. Hang up. Hang up!*

"I got his boxers from under *your* bed, you idiot!" Melody crows. "You really think Rafe would betray you? That moron followed you around like a puppy. He loved you, and you crushed him, and all I had to do was wave a pair of undies in your face!"

As usual, my ex-friend cracks open my chest, rips out my heart, and stomps on it. "What?" I hiss.

"You heard me. You've always been so gullible. Poor Rafe. And he's still chasing you!" Melody snorts. "That's some loyalty there. Maybe I should tell *him* you're dating Damien Blackwood."

I can't breathe. I want to throw up. "You…" My voice trembles with rage. "You…"

"C-U-N-T. I know. But it's oh, so fun messing with you, Little Miss Perfect. Ta-ta!" And Melody hangs up on *me.*

The phone slips from my fingers and onto the floor with a loud clatter. I may have broken it. I don't care.

McKenzy comes out of her room, rubbing her eyes. She pulled an all-nighter working manically on her furniture designs. "What's all the shouting about? Harper, your phone!"

I look down and see the screen has basically shattered. Along with my heart. Tears roll down my cheeks, even though I try to stop them. "I'm so stupid," I whisper.

"Oh, come here. Tell me all about it." She puts an arm around me and gently guides me to the couch.

I can't feel my feet under me, so I'm not even sure how I get there without falling flat on my face. "That was Melody."

"Okay, now I know why there was shouting. What did the fucking bitch want?" McKenzy asks.

My fingers are shaking. I think, idly, how I won't be able to paint with my fingers shaking like this. Then I burst into tears. *What does it matter now?*

"Harper? Harper, talk to me." She rubs my back.

"Melody lied. Rafe never slept with her," I choke out.

Her hand stops. "You're bullshitting me."

"No. But she bullshitted me good for all these years," I reply bitterly.

"That…that…BITCH!" McKenzy wraps her arms around me and holds me tightly. "I'm so sorry, Harper."

"It's my own damn fault for believing her. Oh, God, what am I going to say to Rafe on Friday? I even bought a Green Bay Packers jersey for the occasion. He said in his request I should wear a jersey…"

McKenzy takes a deep breath and encourages me to do the same. "Listen," she says. "Do you have a Vikings jersey?"

"No. Just…" I trail off, a lightbulb going on in my head. "I have the Elk River jersey I stole and never gave back so he'd have to pay for it."

"You do? You didn't burn it?" She gets excited. "Wear it. Wear it to the date!"

I nod. "I'm going to. Maybe he'll see it as an olive branch?"

"Honey, you owe him an olive farm." She sighs, and I know she's right.

"You know what, McKenzy?" I say.

"Yeah?"

"I really hate that bitch."

* * *

Rafe

I was surprised when Harper gave me her real address to pick her up for our date. I was sure she was going to have me pick her up at a dumpster behind a seedy restaurant far from her apartment. Now, I'm in front of the Carleton Artist Lofts, staring at the metal lettering on the brick, and wondering, for the five thousandth time, why I'm even here.

"She's going to come out in a Green Bay jersey," I grumble to myself. "I just know it." As I lean back against my red Ferrari, I watch and wait.

I catch a flash of green in the doorway and brace myself. I've brought a Vikings jersey, just in case she doesn't want to embarrass herself.

The door opens, and out she walks wearing a green and…

…black jersey!

"Holy fuckin' shit!" I gape at her, unable to get out another word as she walks up to me. She stops just shy of me and looks down at the pavement, clenching and unclenching her hands.

"You're wearing my jersey from high school!" I breathe, reaching out to gently play with a sleeve. It's big on her, but then, it always was.

When she looks up, I quickly drop my hand. "Sorry."

"Don't be sorry," she croaks. "I'm sorry."

This is definitely not what I was expecting. Her eyes are red-rimmed and puffy.

"Hey, sugar?" I murmur, tilting her chin up. "What's wrong?"

"Melody told me everything," she blurts. "You were right all along. She was lying!" She covers her face with her hands. "I can't believe I ever believed her. I can't believe I didn't believe *you*."

The information crashes over me like an avalanche. I'm still hurt—angry even—but almost all of that is directed at Melody. It always has been. That bitch.

"Oh, Harper. Come here." I pull her to me and wrap her in a big bear hug.

She grips my shirt and begins bawling just as hard, if not harder, than she did the night we broke up.

"I'm such an idiot." Her voice is muffled by my shirt.

"Hey, she was your friend. What are you gonna do, right?"

"Believe my boyfriend," she replies, her voice cracking.

"Okay, yeah, that could have happened. But we're here now, and we've got it all worked out. I figure we can be friends. I've missed that, you know? Being your friend," I whisper, brushing my fingers over her soft, long hair that cascades down her back.

She even remembered the clips she used to hold her hair back from her face, since I liked her to have it down long but still be able to see her clearly. I smile sadly and rock her in my arms.

"How can you ever forgive me?" She looks up at me, and I remember that old country song "Just to See You Smile."

I brush a lock of hair back over her shoulder, letting it run through my fingers as I do so. "I forgave you a long time ago. Don't cry anymore, okay? You don't need to. It's all okay now."

"Okay." Her voice is still scratchy.

I wipe her tears with my sleeve. "Now, come on. I want you to see my Ferrari."

She gives me a laugh. "You always wanted one."

"I did, and now I've got one. Hop in." I hold the passenger door open for her.

When she slides into the leather seat, my mind begins to race. *Melody confessed. Harper is here. She doesn't hate me anymore!*

To me, the possibilities are endless. I'm not going to play on her guilt, but I am going to show her a good time. The woman I cared so much about is back in my life.

I get behind the wheel and grin at her like the schoolboy I used to be. "Wanna see how fast this thing goes?"

"No!" she protests, and I fight the urge to pout. "You'll get a ticket."

"How about I take you out to the race track someday then?" I suggest. "Give you a good run around there?"

"We have a speedway in Minnesota?" she asks, her nose wrinkling in that cute way that shows off her freckles.

"Yep." I grin at her. "But to get to one able to handle this baby open up, we should probably go to Indy."

Harper looks at me and her eyes are full of apology and… something else. Hope, maybe? "You'd take a trip with me?"

"Harper, I'd go anywhere with you. You know that, right?" I put the Ferrari in gear. Nothing like a manual transmission.

She puts her hand over mine. "I feel the same way," she whispers.

Possibilities I never imagined I'd have again unfurl in my mind with that one touch. "Sugar, baby," I say, threading my fingers through hers. "Let's see if you still know how to drive a stick."

And then we're off.

TEN

Driving a Stick

Harper

It feels just like old times. Except, instead of sitting in a beat-up old Corolla, we're peeling through the city streets in a brand new red Ferrari.

Rafe guides my hand expertly on the stick shift, his hand warm on mine, his strong fingers fitting right where they used to.

"How've you been, Harper?" he asks. "How's the painting going?"

"I just actually had a big break," I reply. 'So, that's been nice. I might be getting busy pretty soon."

"But not too busy to see me." He gives me puppy-dog eyes.

"No," I reply softly. "Not too busy to see you."

He grins as we pull into the parking lot behind a sports bar. It looks like a bit of a dive, but then, he used to like those. Especially when people started to recognize him from college football. These types of places, nobody bothered him.

Rafe takes off his seatbelt, then leans over to undo mine, following it all the way to the other side of my body. I can feel his breath on my cheek. He smells the same, like musk and the same cologne from high school.

I turn my head. He looks at me. I look at him.

Then we're kissing each other hungrily, his hands tangled in my hair, my hands squeezing his strong, sculpted shoulders.

"God damn, sugar. Please tell me we're going to fuck," he pleads.

I unzip his pants. "Lay back."

He's almost bulging out of his boxer-briefs. I scoop his cock free, then firmly grip it at the base. Then I lower my head and lick his tip before taking him down my throat.

"Shit, sugar, you don't have to—" he gasps.

I answer by massaging his shaft with my throat muscles.

Rafe groans and twists his fingers into my hair. "So, this is really happening," he breathes. "Holy fuck."

I intend to blow him better than he's ever been blown before. Even and especially by me. Seeing him again after all these years have reignited the fire that burned inside of me for so long. I loved him. I was going to marry him. Until fucking Melody ruined it all.

I deserve to be intimate with the man I was going to marry, damn it!

"Stop, stop!" Rafe urges, tugging on my hair.

I let his cock go and look up at him. "What's wrong?"

"Not like this. I want to be inside you," he pants, pulling at the hem of the jersey I'm wearing.

I whip it over my head. I wore a camisole underneath just in case the collar slipped down. I didn't want to flash anyone.

He cups my breast through the camisole, rubbing a nipple with his thumb. "Sugar, let me see those beautiful tits."

As I peel up my camisole, he takes my hips and starts kissing every inch of skin as I expose it.

His lips close over a nipple, sucking with just the right pressure, darting his tongue over the peak. My hands spike into his short blond hair.

Rafe moves to the other nipple, and the air feels cool against my wet breast. Then his hands go from stroking my waist and belly to dip below the waistband of my jeans. He unfastens the top button, then slowly draws down my zipper, his knuckles grazing my mound all the way down.

When he lets go of my other nipple, I tug at his shirt, pushing it up to his armpits to expose even more muscle than had been there when we were in school. "Been working out?" I ask, placing my hand over his rock hard abs.

"Gotta stay in tip-top shape in the NFL," he tells me, pulling his shirt the rest of the way off. His hands return to my jeans.

I lift my hips so he can pull them and my cream-colored lace panties off.

"All aboard the Bullet express." He grins, his dick sticking out proudly from his toned body.

It's a bit difficult getting over the gearshift, but Rafe helps me, and then I'm in his lap. I anchor his dick with my hand and slide his cock into my wet pussy, sitting all the way down, taking all of him in.

He keeps his hands on my hips, his eyes closing as he begins thrusting powerfully up into me. "Damn, Harper," he pants.

I put my hands on his muscular pecs and rub all the way down to his washboard abs. God, he's so fucking hot. I might lose myself before I can even get him close.

Rafe laughs a little, then groans when it all becomes too much, and he sends me over the edge. He cums hard inside me, gripping my hips so hard it's clear who is in charge here.

Damn Melody anyway, I think to myself as I lie down on Rafe's chest, breathing hard.

"So… that happened," he wheezes, running his hands up and down my back.

"It sure did," I agree.

His phone rings, but he ignores it, still holding me, still stroking me, still half inside me. I bask in the afterglow.

Until his phone starts pinging insistently with text messages.

"Fuuuuuck," Rafe groans when they don't stop. "Fine, fine. Ugh." Without dislodging me, he wriggles his hand into the pocket of his jeans and pulls out his phone. "It's the guys," he tells me apologetically. "They're wondering where I am."

"Oh. Should we go in?" I ask.

He looks down at his phone again and pales. "I think we'd better. They've spotted the car and said that if I don't get my ass in there in the next few minutes, they're coming out to get me."

"Oh…" I swallow. "You don't think they saw, do you?"

Rafe grins at me. "Tinted windows." He taps the glass.

"Good," I reply, relieved. It's one thing to fuck against floor-to-ceiling windows several stories above the city. Having a bunch of jocks heckle you while you fuck in a car in a parking lot is a whole other story.

He grabs some napkins from the console and we both clean up. I spend a lot of time on my private parts to make sure I don't smell, then he pulls up his boxer-briefs and pants. He helps me get back into my clothes, shoves the nasty napkins in the door, then pats down my hair.

"One more thing," he says before opening the car door. He takes my face in his large hands and kisses me.

Someone bangs on the window, and we spring apart. "Rafe! We know you're in there! Come on, it's your turn to get the tab!" Three big, burly football players surround the car.

"Coming! Coming!" Rafe responds, opening his door. They yank him out and start jostling him around, the usual team stuff. "Guys, guys," he finally calls. "My girl is in there. I need to introduce her to you.

All eyes turn back to the car.

I blush with embarrassment as Rafe walks around to open the passenger door and gives me his hand.

"They're nice guys," he assures me softly. "Relax. We'll all have a good time."

Once he's pulled me out of the car, Rafe drops his arm around my shoulders. "Guys, this is Harper. Harper, these are the guys."

"Some of them anyway," one chuckles. He looks me up and down, then extends his hand. "Beau."

I shake his hand. "Nice to meet you," I say politely.

The others introduce themselves, then sweep us into the sports bar. There are various games playing on every screen, mostly hokey, but also one TV with soccer, two with golf, and, surprisingly, one with a poker tournament.

"Is that really considered a sport?" I ask the guys.

Beau shrugs. "I figure if you can bet on it, it must be a sport."

They all laugh, and I get caught up in the camaraderie. Beer flows freely, except Rafe doesn't drink any.

"Can't be jeopardizing my sugar's life," he says by way of explanation when I look down at his third Coke.

I feel a soft spot in my heart. I'm his sugar again.

Then I remember I am also Damien's little red bird, and Scott's… well, I don't think he has a pet name for me yet, but I'm going to be his *something. Oh God, oh God. How am I supposed to navigate this?*

"What's wrong, Harper?" Rafe asks, noting my distress.

"I… um… I'm…" I rub the back of my neck. "I'm sort of seeing other people right now too. And I don't know what you're going to think about it, but I don't want to lie to you either."

Rafe arches an eyebrow at me. He pulls me away to a private corner. "How many other people?"

I swallow. "Um… two." I brace myself, wondering what I'm going to do if he gets mad. Looking inward, I just don't want to let go of Damien. Or Scott, for that matter. This is new and uncharted territory for me, but if Rafe refuses to accept this new lifestyle I'm exploring, sadly, I will have to let him go.

To my surprise, Rafe grins. "Awesome! I knew you had it in you to go against those stodgy, religious old farts and live a little."

"You are talking about my parents," I try to scold him, but laugh instead. I'm so relieved.

"Yeah. The stodgy old farts," he repeats unrepentantly.

"You are impossible!" I give him a light punch to the shoulder.

"Careful, that's my throwing arm. You don't want to take out the quarterback before the season even starts, do you?"

"Your arm's insured." But I lean forward and kiss it just the same. "Feel better?"

Rafe nods. "Much."

A great weight has been lifted off my shoulder. But without that boulder weighing me down, I am suddenly exhausted.

He looks back at his teammates, then at me. "You wanna get the fuck out of here?"

"Yeah. I need to get home. McKenzy's on pins and needles waiting for me to tell her how our date went." I yawn. "And I don't think I'll be much fun from now on."

"You don't need to be fun. You just need to be you." He smiles. Then we weave our way back through the bar and say our goodbyes.

In the Ferrari, I hold Rafe's hand on the stick-shift again. This time, he drives slowly and definitely takes the long way around.

When we finally get to the apartment, he opens my door for me again. "I'd invite you up, but you'd definitely need to come in a different car for that in this neighborhood. I can't assure you no one would fuck with this one if you left it on the street."

"I do like the Ferrari…" He grins at me. "It'd be worth it, though." We get out of the car, and Rafe makes a face, and a pungent smell hits me at the same time. "Those are some nasty cigarettes someone's smoking."

"Yeah." They remind me of my most recent ex, but I don't want to think about him now. I go up on my toes and kiss him on the lips. "Call me, or text me. But for God's sake, don't buy me again!"

"I was going to ask you about that," he remembers. "Why *are* you on a pay-to-date site? Are you a sugar baby?"

I groan. "No. I really have to get off that site, and I will this weekend. McKenzy signed me up because I was having trouble selling my artwork. But I can't get off just yet. It's just that this guy Tomás messaged me and told me how his wife cheated on him, and he needs a younger woman on his arm when he goes to his niece's quinceañera because she's going to be there—"

"Say no more. I know how soft-hearted you are." His eyebrows draw together in confusion. "I'm sorry you had to do that in the first place."

"Starving artist," I admit. "Like I said, it was McKenzy's idea. But it panned out pretty well."

"And you don't need any more money? Because, suddenly, I've got loads of it," Rafe offers.

I kiss him again. "No. I just need you."

He goes all soft and squishy for a second, then clears his throat. "Okay. I'll call you. Love ya, sugar."

Rafe is in the Ferrari before I can get my mouth working again. There's a suspicious lump in my throat.

Though he doesn't expect me to say it back, and he can't hear me anyway, I whisper, "I love you, Rafe."

ELEVEN

Three Men and Counting

Harper

Scott Bauer: Hey, Harper. What are you doing this weekend?

I roll over and look at my phone. My adrenaline spikes with both excitement and trepidation. It's Scott!

We haven't corresponded all week, and this is the first time I'm realizing it. I am such a bad girlfriend.

Potential *girlfriend.*

Hey, wait, why hasn't *he* texted *me* before now?

I might be a little indignant, actually.

Harper Ward: Hey, stranger. How've you been?

Scott Bauer: Missing you. *cheese emoji*

I laugh.

Harper Ward: LOL, liar. You been busy?

Scott Bauer: *pouty face emoji* I really have missed you. But yeah, busy. Some asshole crop duster was a little off on his aim and sprayed pesticides on a small area of the farm.

I wince, and text back quickly.

Harper Ward: Oh, Scott, I'm so sorry. That sucks big time.

Scott Bauer: Yeah, well, I had to rip out that crop. It's all fixed now. I was wondering if you are busy on Sunday.

I have to think about that. With Rafe, and now Tomás, taking up so much time I really ought to dedicate a day to painting.

Then again, this is Scott. I haven't seen him all week, and I need to tell him about my lifestyle change.

I decide I can paint during the week.

Scott Bauer: Harper?

Harper Ward: Sorry! Sorry. I would love to get together on Sunday. Want me to drive out to the farm?

Scott Bauer: You have a car?

Harper Ward: Well, I share it with McKenzy, but she doesn't need it for anything that day.

Scott Bauer: I'd love it if you came out to the farm! *happy emoji*

I laugh. Who knew Scott was such an emoji man?

Harper Ward: What, no eggplant emoji?

Scott Bauer: I would never! *eggplant emoji*

Harper Ward: LOL, okay, mister, it's a date.

Scott Bauer: *confetti emoji* See you around four?

Harper Ward: Absolutely!

Scott Bauer: *kissy face emoji*

I set my phone aside and sit up, rubbing my eyes. Then I realize it's already past noon! I scramble up and into the shower, leaving my phone on the counter. It dings just as I'm conditioning my hair.

Wincing with one eye closed, I reach outside the curtain to grab it.

Damien Blackwood: Are you available for dinner this coming Friday?

I smile. Damien. A man of few words who gets right to the point. I'm taking down my At a Loose End profile after Tomás tonight, so Friday seems like a great idea.

Harper Ward: You give some good notice. Yes, I'd love to have dinner with you on Friday.

Damien Blackwood: All right. Pick you up at 7:00 PM. I'll send a dress. Have fun with Tomás tonight.

My jaw drops.

Harper Ward: STALKER!!!

Damien Blackwood: You love it.

The truth is, I kind of do. He isn't a creeper, just a man who likes to be in-the-know.

Harper Ward: I'm taking my profile down tomorrow after payment goes through.

Damien Blackwood: Far be it for me to tell you what to do, but I like that idea. If I share you with too many men, then I won't be able to see you as often as I'd like, little red bird.

This is the most he's ever texted me, which makes me think maybe he really does like me.

Harper Ward: With you, that's three, total. But I guess you probably knew that already.

Damien Blackwood: Is Rafe all right with the arrangement? A little birdy told me you used to be engaged.

Harper Ward: Not this birdy! But yes, he's actually excited for me. I'm a rebel now!

Damien Blackwood: As every good artist should be. All right, I'll talk to you soon.

Harper Ward: Later!

I put my phone back down and rinse out my hair. I turban it on top of my head as I step out of the shower. I'm just reaching for my lilac lotion when my phone goes off again.

It's a number I don't recognize with the simple message, "I'm assuming you blocked my other number, sugar?"

I blush and quickly put the lotion down to fumble with my phone.

Harper Ward: Maaaaybe

Rafe Maloney: This is my new number.

Harper Ward: Good thing too! We never got around to exchanging numbers last night.

Rafe Maloney: We were busy. *eggplant, peach, water squirt* *winky face*

Harper Ward: RAFE!!!

Rafe Maloney: Yeah, I remember that too.

Harper Ward: *eye roll emoji* You are completely incorrigible!

Rafe Maloney: Don't use big words, sugar. My head might explode.

Harper Ward: You were fourth in our graduating class, and were doing even better in college when we broke up, so don't you try to go all meathead on me!

Rafe Maloney: Lol. I just wanted to say I miss you and to thank you for last night, and not just for the car sex.

I laugh and shake my head at my phone, even though he can't see it.

Harper Ward: You really are completely shameless.

Rafe Maloney: You love that about me.

I look around the bathroom as though someone might jump out and catch me. Then I send it.

Harper Ward: *red heart emoji*

Rafe Maloney: I think I just came.

What?

Harper Ward: Oh my God you *poop emoji* I was trying to express my feelings!

Rafe Maloney: Relax, sugar. I love you too See you Thursday.

I frown in confusion. Did I miss something last night?

Harper Ward: What are we doing Thursday?

Rafe Maloney: Hopefully me.

I let out a shriek of laughter and indignation.

Harper Ward: RAFE!!!

Rafe Maloney: HARPER!!!

Harper Ward: Ugh. Fine, see you Thursday.

Rafe Maloney: Looking forward to it.

The bathroom door opens, and McKenzy sticks her head in. "Are you okay? I heard screaming."

"Oh, just one of my men acting up." I reach for my lotion with a smile on my face.

She gives me a conspiratorial wink. "I like the sound of that. 'One of my men.' I might try that out someday."

"Yeah, well, be ready for a *very* full schedule!" I reply, lotioning up my legs.

"You make that sound like a threat." She giggles then closes the bathroom door behind her.

I finish in the bathroom within the next twenty minutes and go sit on my bed, balancing my laptop on my knees.

"Okay, Internet. Help a girl out," I mutter, typing into the search bar.

What to wear to a quinceañera?

The search engine very helpfully compiles a few ideas. I look at some pictures, my eyebrows hitting my hairline. I didn't realize it was such a formal event!

"Cocktail dress." *Shit, do I even own one of those?*

I close my laptop and slide off the bed. "Uh… McKenzy…?"

My bestie comes out of her bedroom holding two cocktail dresses. One is a muted pink. One is an emerald green.

"You really are scary sometimes," I chuckle, walking over and taking the pink form-fitting strapless number. I am supposed to be out-doing an ex-wife, after all.

"I knew you'd get around to looking up what you're supposed to wear far too late for you to go out and get a dress." She winks at me. "Do I know my girl or what?"

I hold the dress up and realize the tag is still on it. "Oh, my God, McKenzy! Did you go out and buy this for me?"

"Last Monday," she confirms. "What, you think my curvy ass was going to fit into that? If I gave you one of my dresses, the top would fall down, and your boobs would pop out!"

"Fair," I reply. I am not as chesty as she is, nor do I have as big of a round booty, but I'm pretty sure I can still be eye candy enough on Tomás' arm to give his ex-wife angina. "I owe you. For both. I'm keeping that green one. You never know."

"You never know," she agrees. "I'll leave the receipts on the counter. You get to it when you get to it."

I smile. It must be nice to have rich, supportive parents. "Thanks, McKenzy. You're the best friend a girl could ever ask for."

"You remember that when my birthday comes around, Miss Famous Painter. I wear a size three-carat emerald," she teases.

"I'll remember," I promise. I take the dress into my room and spend the rest of the afternoon primping.

When I walk back out, I have a half-up, half-down hairstyle held in place by my grandmother's silver comb. The dress fits me like Saran wrap, but not in a slutty way. I'm wearing a strapless, push-up bra. I know I don't have to, the bodice of the dress is stiff enough to wrangle my boobs, but I really want to make this woman green for Tomás.

McKenzy has already resurrected the silver strappy sandals from the wedding I attended with Scott. She's placed them just outside my door.

"I wonder where she's gone off to," I murmur, opening my silver clutch and checking my phone.

No texts.

Weird.

I slip the shoes on and buckle them then glance at my phone again for the time.

6:20 PM

God, I'm good! I smile to myself.

I go down the elevator to the lobby, then out the front door, where there are two tan cars parked. One is a Ford, the other a Volvo.

Well, crap. Which one is it? I start walking toward the Ford, but it slowly pulls away from the curb and drives away. I'm pretty sure its window tint is illegally dark for Minnesota.

The driver's door opens on the Volvo, and a man in nice linen pants, a white shirt, and a matching linen jacket steps out.

I stop dead in my tracks.

"Professor García del Rio?" I gape.

My Spanish 1002 professor smiles sheepishly at me. "I thought it might be you, Helena."

Helena. My chosen Spanish name for his class. "Oh, my God! It's been years!" I go over and give him a hug. "I'm sorry to hear about your wife. Isn't she another professor at the university?"

Tomás wraps his arms around me. With my high-heeled shoes on, I'm maybe one inch taller than my Guatemalan former instructor. He buries his face in my shoulder and heaves a sigh. "Thank you. *Sí*. Carmen is another Spanish professor."

"That must make department meetings fun," I say sympathetically. "Wow, I mean, I'm glad it's you, but I'm also sorry it's you. I always liked you and thought you seemed so happy."

Tomás clears his throat. "We were. Until that *pendejo* Alex Bridges from the dental school showed up—with my wife—in my bed."

"Did you… did you come home early or something?" I ask carefully.

"No. She wanted me to catch her. They… um… laughed at me. Then she told me to pack my belongings and get out of my own house." Tomás takes a step back and looks me up and down. "But look at you! All grown up and ready to face the world."

"Ready to face Carmen," I reply with confidence. "You watch. Together, we're going to make her face slide right off."

Tomás bites his lip. "Can I ask you a small favor, Helena?"

"You can call me Harper if you want, though I do still like Helena." I smile. "And sure, ask me anything."

"Could you maybe pull your neckline down another inch and your skirt up another two inches?" he asks, his cheeks flushing with the request.

Grinning, I shimmy the top of the cocktail dress down as far as it will go without exposing the push-up bra, giving him an eyeful. Then I slowly pull the skirt up *three* inches. The dress is very forgiving and drapes nicely, despite my having messed with it.

He swallows, his eyes alternating between my legs and my chest. "*Gracias*."

I kiss him on the cheek. "*De nada, Professor*."

"Ah, you remember some of your Spanish!" Tomás beams. "Please, call me Tomás. And I will call you Helena, if you don't mind. That way, I won't get mixed up."

"Whatever you say, Tomás."

TWELVE

Envy Green

Tomás

¿Ella está aquí para mí? I couldn't believe who I was seeing. Helena, perhaps the most dedicated, intelligent, beautiful student I've ever had the pleasure of teaching, had walked up to *my* car. I thought for a moment she'd been heading for the tan Ford, but no. Helena is my date.

Helena is my date!

I have to keep checking that she's here next to me in my Volvo. It's just surreal.

Helena puts her hand on my thigh. *Mi chile* is not immune to this, even though I know it's meant to be a comforting gesture. I mean, the most sexy woman that I've ever seen has her hand six inches from my *huevos.* "I'm here, and I'm going to be right here the whole time, Tomás."

Of course. I need to remember she's doing this as a favor for me because of Carmen.

Por Dios, I hate that woman. Sitting there, naked, on my bed with that *pendejo* she'd been fucking who knew how long behind my back, telling me to grab my shit and get out. Walking in with

Helena on my arm is going to be a boost to my ego, and hopefully, a slam to hers.

I drive us out to Fridley, where my brother has rented the Grand Olympian Ballroom from Banquets of Minnesota. The whole time, I'm trying very hard not to stare at her legs and her chest. I didn't pay much attention, as a married man, but as a man with red blood in his veins, I did note she was stunning in a university sweatshirt and a perky ponytail back when she was in my class. However, now that I'm single and she's in—*Dios* help me—that dress? She's a *bombón.*

My brother is outside greeting guests when we arrive. He's already giving me an apologetic look as I pull up to let Helena out. Then his eyes shift to her, and he takes a step back, his mouth opening wide enough to catch flies.

Pride swells in me, then other things, when Helena squeezes my thigh once more. "See? One down…"

"Four hundred to go," I reply, my voice strained with desire. But I tamp it down. Helena's just doing me this favor. It's nothing more than that.

Her head whips around, and I catch her lilac scent again. "Four hundred?"

"Give or take. Large, Hispanic Catholic family," I say.

She squares her shoulders. "Well, four-hundred people are about to know you're a total stud."

My brother comes to the passenger door, still blinking as though blinded by a ray of sunlight, and opens it, offering Helena his hand. "*Buenas noches,* Miss…?"

"Oh, you can just call me Helena." She giggles perfectly, tossing her hair over her shoulder before taking Ernesto's hand.

"H-Helena," he jibbers, helping her out of my Volvo. "What a pretty name."

"Thanks!" She turns to me and gives me a subtle wink. "*Mi amor,*" she continues in a perfect accent, "don't be long. I'll miss you too much."

I give her a goofy smile. I am in so much trouble. "I will be right back, *mi preciosa.* I just need to park the car."

"I'll park the car," Ernesto surprises me by volunteering. At my frown, when he comes around to the driver's side, he says, "Carmen is already here. *Por favor*, wait for me before you go say hello. I wouldn't miss this for the world."

"I still don't know why Julieta invited her." I grumble but step out of the car so he can get behind the wheel.

"They used to shop together. Nostalgia? Denial? *No sé*. What I do know is I'm asking Bruno to film this for posterity," he chuckles. Then he pulls away.

I walk up next to Helena, and she quickly attaches herself to my arm, close enough to be a barnacle. Except her lovely breast is soft against my arm that my mouth goes dry.

"I'm here," she says again, and I realize she's mistaken my lusty discomfort for something else. She thinks I'm worried about Carmen. I'm starting to worry more about my pants, but there is no way I'm telling her that. Having her plastered to me, soft, lilac-scented, beautiful, is the best thing that's happened to me in years.

Ernesto jogs up, clearly quite serious about seeing this moment I'm about to have with Carmen. "*Estoy listo*. Let me just text Bruno quickly. Then we can go inside."

Go inside. Now I'm starting to sweat. Even with Helena hanging on me, I don't know how I'm going to feel when I see Carmen with Alex Bridges. I know he's her date. Ernesto warned me ahead of time.

Helena kisses my cheek then brushes her lips over my neck. I can't breathe for a moment, wondering what she's doing, when I realize she's getting lipstick on the collar of my shirt.

"You play in a whole different league," I breathe.

"It's all for you," she whispers in my ear. "You're a handsome, intelligent, honest, good-hearted man, and you deserve to rub her face in her own stink."

I smile and stand a bit straighter. It doesn't even bother me that Helena might be my height or taller in her heels. She makes me feel taller than the tallest building. "Whenever you're ready, Ernesto."

"He's on it. Let's go," my brother says.

We walk into the reception hall to the sight of white-covered chairs and long tables that will be moved back later to make room for dancing. Flowers are everywhere. My niece Julieta has chosen purple as her theme color to intersperse among the white. Several shades of lavender pop everywhere.

"It's beautiful," Helena compliments Ernesto. "You and your wife are very generous parents. Did I miss the mass?"

"I think you would have given *el padre* a heart attack if you'd been at the mass with Tomás," my brother replies. "Don't worry. Tomás wasn't there either. He and *el padre* have a difference of opinion over saving his marriage."

Helena arches one perfectly-sculpted eyebrow. "There's something there to save?"

"You know the Catholic church. Or perhaps you don't?" he asks.

"My parents are very religious Christians. But tonight, I'll be as Catholic as you like." She smiles back.

Ernesto throws his head back and laughs. "Oh, I like her," he says to me.

I can't help it. I feel the soft, goofy grin settling on my face again as I look at Helena. "I do too."

Her gaze is soft on me as well, and for just a moment, I wonder if tonight might not be the only night I get to have her on my arm.

Julieta is greeting guests. She is resplendent in a wide-skirted white dress decorated with little purple flowers in many shades. She has a purple sash around her waist as well, tied in a bow in the back, and purple and white flowers in her dark hair. When she sees me, she squeals and rushes over. "*¡Tío Tomás!* I'm so glad you came."

Her enthusiasm confuses me, as I'm sure she knew I might not come if Carmen did, but she invited her anyway. "Julieta, you look like a princess. Oh! Before I forget." I pull a card with a not insubstantial amount of money in it out of my jacket and hand it to her. "For you."

"*Gracias, tío Tomás,*" she replies, putting the card in a little purse dangling from her wrist. I have no doubt there is the better part of a college fund in there by now. Then she looks over at my date, and her expression goes through so many contortions within a split second that I wonder if she's sprained a facial muscle. "*¿Quién es ella?*"

"Oh. I'm sorry, how rude of me. Julieta, this is Helena. Helena, this is Julieta, my niece and the quinceañera," I introduce.

Helena holds out her hand, just as confused about Julieta's unreadable expression as I am.

Julieta then grins and grasps Helena's hand in both of hers. "I feel bad now, inviting Carmen. I mean, I felt bad as soon as she showed up with Alex. I thought maybe you two could make up tonight, but I was so wrong, *tío Tomás*. But this makes it better." Her smile turns mischievous. "Is there any way you could pull your skirt up a little higher, Miss Helena?"

Ernesto scolds Julieta. Or tries to. The problem is, we're all laughing too hard for it to really stick.

Helena winks and pulls her skirt up one more inch. Another three inches, and I'll be able to see what color of panties she's wearing.

"You're the best!" Julieta kisses her on either cheek. "Enjoy the party. I'm just sorry I won't see the fireworks."

"Your brother is going to be recording," Ernesto says.

"Fantastic!" Julieta looks past us to see other guests arriving. "I'll be sure to see you later. Good luck!"

"With legs like those, they won't need any luck," my brother chuckles. He points subtly to one of the tables, in front of which are standing Carmen and Alex.

I take a deep breath. "Here goes nothing."

Helena snuggles even closer to me than before, which I hadn't thought was possible. "Lead on, Tomás."

* * *

HARPER

I can see the dark-haired woman with red highlights in her hair standing in a green, barely-decent cocktail dress next to a gray-haired white man in a suit. I remember her from Spanish 1022. She was a real bitch. I'm glad my initial impressions of her were correct. Everybody likes to be right sometimes.

Tomás walks over with his head held high and me slinking along on his arm. I lean up to whisper in his ear as we approach.

"Oh, Tommy," I say, loud enough for Carmen and Alex to hear, but not loud enough to bust my *profesor's* eardrums. "You didn't tell me she had such a cute little pooch!"

Tomás coughs while Carmen, who has yet to say a word, turns red as the crystal punch bowl on a nearby table.

"Tommy?" Alex echoes, looking as though his balding, poochie ass is going to mix it up with the lean, fit Tomás until he realizes the obvious discrepancy and backs down with a hunch to his shoulders. "I guess we haven't seen you since Carmen threw you out, 'Tommy.'"

Carmen recovers and gives a catty smile. "How is that fleabag motel you're staying in?"

Oh, bitch goin' *down*. Before Tomás can answer, I widen my eyes and say, "I wasn't really paying attention to the decor, *Señora Carmen*. If you know what I mean." I giggle again. "Oh, but you must. I don't know how a woman your age kept up! I'm glad you're with someone now who's more your speed." I cuddle Tomás' arm. "Tommy's a very naughty professor."

Tomás chokes, then smiles fondly at me. "Helena and I are still in the honeymoon phase," he apologizes to Carmen and Alex. "We just can't seem to keep our hands off each other."

To emphasize his point, I slide my hand across his chest and under his lapel, right over his nipple. I feel it harden through the thin fabric of his dress shirt.

Hmm. Interesting. Much to my surprise, I start getting ideas about my naughty professor. Ideas I really shouldn't be having while I'm dating three men at once. I mean, would it even be possible to add a fourth? Is Tomás even ready for another relationship after Carmen burned him so badly?

I blink. Tomás and I are still staring into each other's eyes.

"Ugh, get a room," Alex grunts. His eyes are on my legs. Then my tits. Then my legs. He licks his lips, and I suddenly feel very creeped out. Maybe I shouldn't have hiked my dress up that last inch.

Carmen clears her throat noisily. She hasn't missed the once, twice, maybe sixteen-overs Alex has given my body.

"He's gross," I murmur to Tomás, unable to suppress a shiver of revulsion.

Tomás steps just in front of me. "I don't think it's polite to ogle. Especially when you've got another woman on your arm."

Alex splutters his wine, and Tomás and I are far enough away not to get splattered, but spit and wine, stain Carmen's green dress.

She shrieks, pushes Alex hard in the chest, and starts for the door. "Take me home, Alex!" she demands as they walk off. "And don't think you're staying over." I can just barely hear her from across the room.

I'm afraid we've ruined Julieta's quinceañera by accident, but the guest of honor is covering her mouth, her shoulders shaking with laughter. Ernesto, and who I can only assume is Bruno, high-five each other from a nearby corner.

Tomás isn't even watching Carmen's exit. He spins me around into his arms and kisses me passionately.

I'm panting by the time we part. I've never had a kiss that spicy before.

"What about Carmen?" I ask anxiously, knowing we're headed down a completely new path.

"Who's Carmen?" Tomás replies. And kisses me again.

THIRTEEN

The Naughty Professor

Tomás

I'm sure Carmen's humiliation was masterful and her exit the perfect end to a toxic relationship. I was only tertiarily aware of it, however. As soon as that disgusting *cerdo* of a man began eye-fucking Helena, I was only aware of the blood rushing in my ears.

It's a good thing Alex is a dentist, because if they hadn't left when they did, I was going to knock his teeth out. "I'm sorry, Helena. I didn't expect that man would be such a pig."

She slides her hand into mine and squeezes it. "I kind of did, so don't worry about it."

I bring her hand to my lips and kiss it. "You were spectacular."

"You weren't even paying attention," she replies shrewdly.

"No." I brush my fingers through the hair at the back of her neck, the part she's left down. "I wasn't." I lean close to her.

She cups my cheeks, kisses me, and the world gets lost again.

Someone clears their throat, and I grumpily look up. It's Ernesto.

"Sorry to disturb," he grins, "but I think you should probably let Helena eat before whatever you have planned tonight."

Whatever I have planned? I glance back at Helena, who is biting her kiss-swollen bottom lip. Her eyes are dilated with desire, and I find myself making all kinds of plans. Well, mostly thinking about positions. This quinceañera can't end soon enough.

"I suppose I should feed you." I smile and wrap my arm around her waist, holding her close as we walk.

"I suppose you should," Helena agrees. "I have a feeling I might need the energy."

I wait until we're out of Ernesto's hearing range then whisper, "Count on it."

We eat. Helena talks to other people around us, smiling and laughing, and I nod along with the conversations, though I have no idea what they're about. All I can think about is that, as soon as this is over, my cock going to be buried inside her.

¡Mierda! My brain suddenly arrives at the fact that I don't have condoms.

"What's the matter? she asks me, catching my expression.

"I don't have protection," I murmur in her ear, frustrated. "We're going to have to stop at a gas station or something."

She gives me a grin. "I have an IUD.".

I get to have her with nothing between us? I need to get out of here now, but there's still the father-daughter dance.

Helena, oblivious to my predicament, turns back to my tía Margarita. I think they're talking about recipes for *pepián.*

Then I feel Helena's hand on my thigh. *Fuck, I'm not gonna make it!*

Her hand moves upward, under the napkin in my lap, to my straining fly.

I have plenty of time to stop her but I don't. Not when she cups me through my pants or when she eases my zipper down. Not even when she reaches into my boxers and takes my cock in her hand. She's talking about potatoes now. And *huiskil.* The whole time, she's jerking me off.

I keep nodding along as though I'm paying attention. Her hand feels perfect around my dick. She uses just the right pressure. I know it won't be long before I cum.

The only concession I make to decency before I explode in her hand is to maneuver the napkin to catch the thick stream that pulses out of me.

Biting the inside of my cheek against a shout of pleasure, I squeeze Helena's thigh while she finishes cleaning me up. I drop the napkin on the floor, under the floor-length tablecloth. I'll grab it and throw it in the trash before we go. Cloth or not, I'm not letting some poor, unsuspecting soul grab that particular napkin.

When the world comes back into focus, I have a wicked thought.

I take the hand on her thigh and begin peeling up her skirt.

* * *

HARPER

I know exactly what he's going to do the second his fingers trail up my thigh, pushing my skirt out of the way. My heart pounds, and I quickly grab his wrist when he reaches my panties.

Tomás pauses, then leans close and whispers in my ear. "Do you really want me to stop?" His breath is warm in my ear. It sends a tingle down my spine.

I don't want him to stop.

I let go of his wrist. He presses a chaste kiss to my bare shoulder then changes the subject with his aunt.

I can't imagine he grasped much of the conversation I'd been having with her, but now I'm the one who barely knows what's going on. He runs his fingers in a featherlight touch between my legs, no doubt finding me wet through my panties.

"Are things hot and wet in México right now?" Tomás asks his aunt oh-so-innocently.

It takes everything in me not to swat him. "Tomás!" I protest.

"Yes, darling?" he replies, his eyes twinkling with mischief. He leans close again. "Scoot your hips forward and spread your legs more. Then lean back and enjoy, *mi tesoro.*"

"Your aunt…" I try to remind him.

One of the younger cousins approaches our table. "Tía Margarita? Would you like to dance?" he asks.

"You didn't mind my aunt when you were milking my cock," Tomás whispers back.

This is true. I am guilty of getting this man off under the table right in front of his aunt.

Tía Margarita goes with the cousin, leaving us alone at our table. "Well?" Tomás asks.

I scoot my hips forward, spread my legs, and lean back.

"*Bueno*." He flicks the lacy underwear over my entrance aside like a bothersome spiderweb then delves deep with two of his thick fingers.

"Not even a warm-up?" I gasp, my legs flopping open even wider to admit his digits fully.

"My darling, you don't need a warm-up," he tells me.

He's not wrong. As he circles his thumb around my clit, he gives me the finger-fucking of a lifetime. I squeak and bite my lip when he finds just the right spot.

Then he's merciless.

"Mmm, *mi preciosa*, you suck my fingers in so well," he whispers. "I will remember this spot, when I am finally inside your beautiful body."

I tremble inside, and he kisses me, the same explosive, mind-numbing kiss he gave me before, just as I come around his fingers. I cling to his shoulders while he sees me all the way through, right to the last little shiver.

"Fuck." He sighs against my lips. "When will this party be over?"

"Not soon enough," I pant, leaning against him as he puts me back together.

The DJ then announces the father-daughter dance.

"Are we leaving after this?" I ask, taking a long swig from a glass of ice water.

"Yes, we are."

After I get my breath back, I give Tomás a sly smile. "You really are naughty, Professor."

He swallows, looking at the condensation that's dripped from the glass and onto my chest. "You know," he says thoughtfully. "I've always wanted to do that."

"What?" I ask.

"Fuck a student in my office," he confesses. "Of course, it would be completely inappropriate. I never even fucked my wife in there."

"Oh." I give him a soft kiss. "Sounds like your desk needs to be taken for its maiden voyage."

Tomás swallows. "You'd really do that? Let me fuck you on my desk?"

"Sounds like a plan to me." I grin. "I mean, I've never done that before, but it sounds fun. As long as I don't end up with an imprint of your name plate on my ass."

He laughs, but it's tight with nervousness and desire.

The father-daughter dance ends.

We clap.

Tomás pulls me to my feet, takes a look at me, then puts his jacket around me. It smells spicy and exotic. Like him.

"We made a bit of a wet spot on the back of your dress," he explains with a rueful look.

"It's wash and wear. And even if it isn't, it was worth it," I reply, hugging his jacket around me.

Together, we walk over to his niece and Ernesto. "*Discúlpame,* Julieta, but we need to leave," Tomás says. "It's been such a lovely quinceañera party."

"Thank you for coming! Helena and I need to go shopping soon," Julieta beams.

"I would love to," I respond.

Ernesto and Tomás share a conspiratorial look, but at this point, I don't care who knows the obvious reason he and I are leaving. I'm too hot and bothered for all that.

Tomás puts an arm around my waist and guides me outside. He gives me a soft kiss. "I'll go get the car. You stay right here."

"Okay." I wait for him in the dim light of the street lamps. A cop car drives by slowly, and I wonder if the party has had a noise complaint. The car doesn't stop, so I dismiss it.

The Volvo pulls up, and Tomás scrambles out to open the

passenger door for me. It's adorable. I stroke his cheek and give him a lingering kiss.

"Helena," he breathes against my lips.

I love that he's still using my old Spanish class name. "*Profe*," I tease.

"Say that when I make you come on my desk," Tomás requests.

"I can do that," I reply.

He helps me into the car then closes the door carefully.

From door to door, it takes less than twenty-five minutes. Tomás parks in staff parking near the building where his office is then takes my hand and guides me down to the basement where the Spanish faculty offices are. His office is still in the same place it was seven years ago. It makes me smile. He fumbles a bit with the keys, but we're soon inside his office. The desk is piled high with test booklets.

"Some things never change," I say.

He blushes. "I wish I could sweep all these onto the floor, but…"

"Relax. It doesn't have to be like the movies. Let me help you." We move test booklets into careful piles on the other side of the room. Then he goes about making sure there aren't any staple fragments, paperclips, or other debris on his desktop. He sees his nameplate and quickly dumps it in his desk.

Then he looks at me. "Still game?" he asks.

Feeling bold, I walk up to him and cup him through his pants. "What do you think?" I drop his jacket over the back of his office chair and kick off my shoes.

He pulls me against him then unzips my dress and lets it fall to the floor. My strapless push-up bra goes next, then my panties. For a moment, he just stares at my body. Then he lifts me onto the desktop.

"Are you going to teach me something today, *Profe*?" I ask, batting my eyelashes.

He takes off his clothes, and his thick dick springs out. "Yes," he says in an instructive tone. "Today, we're learning about multiple orgasms."

FOURTEEN

A Lesson in Orgasms

Harper

"Lie back," Tomás tells me, and I lay down on the cold, hard surface of his desk. It's kinda hot.

He leans over me, pressing his palms to the desktop on either side of me. "God, you are so beautiful," he whispers, kissing my shoulder. He latches onto my nipple next, and I whimper, gripping the edge of the desk and arching my back.

"*Profe*," I beg. "I'm ready. Please, fuck me."

Tomás groans and one hand disappears behind the desk. He lines his head up to press against my entrance. While he's still sucking my nipple, he starts to push inside of me.

He's so wide. Not as long as Scott, but definitely thicker, if that's even possible. He stretches me wall to wall and I throw my head back, gasping as he goes in to the hilt.

"Do you like that?" he asks.

As if I'm going to tell him no! "*Sí, profe*," I reply.

"Do you want more?" he asks me.

Fuck yes I want more! "Please!" moan.

He starts to thrust, his lips latching onto my other nipple.

And I thought his kisses were explosive. His mouth should come with a warning label, I swear! "*Más, profe,*" I say, asking for more.

"So hungry," Tomás tsks, teasing me by fucking me slower rather than faster.

"*¡Profe!*" I protest.

"Shh, I'm gonna stuff you full soon. Patience." He continues at an unhurried pace, tasting my skin everywhere with little nibbles and licks like I'm cotton candy.

I want him to consume me. I want his big dick to destroy me. I reach out and stroke his cheek, making him look up. "*Please?*" I all but whine. "*Por favor, Profe.*"

Tomás kisses my wrist. "I'll give you what you need." Then he draws his hips back and slams them forward, making me cry out. He does it again. And again.

His dick rubs right where I need it with every hard stroke—hell, it's so wide and it stretches me so much I can hardly breathe, but it feels so good. I make sounds not yet recorded by science and start to see sparks at the edges of my vision.

"Come for me, Helena," Tomás says, and I do. I come hard around his wide dick.

But he doesn't finish. He keeps going.

"*¿P-Profe?*" I gasp as he grips my hips and fucks me harder. I grab the edge of the desk just over my head and hang on for dear life.

"Helena…" Tomás groans. "I need more. It's been so long…."

I had no idea how Carmen ever thought of giving this up to be with a dentist. But now I'm really confused. How long had she been holding out on him?

Bitch.

Well, I'm getting the benefit of her stupidity. Maybe I should write her a thank you card. I moan beneath him. "Take what you need, *Profe.* As many times as you need it. You feel so good."

Tomás grunts and rubs my clit, pressing against it with his shaft with every pass.

I can't help myself. I come again. "*¡Profe!*"

"Fuck!" His hot cum empties into me in strong spurts.

We both pant. Tomás leans down and lays his cheek on my breast. After a moment, he lifts his head and begins to lick my nipple. "I get the impression we're going again?" I ask after a long silence during which we both come down. Well, I come down anyway. His dick is just as hard as ever. I can feel it against my thigh.

"You'd better believe it," he replies, and pulls me into a mind-blowing kiss.

* * *

I SIT in the passenger seat of the Volvo, feeling completely satisfied. Tomás drives, but with a hand on my bare thigh. I know we've just barely satiated his appetite, but after the fourth time he came, I just couldn't keep up anymore.

"Next time, I won't be so needy," he promises me, giving me a sideways glance. There's a lot loaded in that one sentence.

"Next time?" I tease.

He clears his throat. "I hate to be presumptuous, but I am hoping there's a next time."

I take a deep breath and put my hand over his on my thigh, threading our fingers together. "You need to know I'm dating three other guys. It's only fair for you to understand that."

Tomás pauses a while then squeezes my thigh and nods. "*Mi preciosa*, you are far too sweet not to share."

"That's okay with you?" I ask tentatively.

"Sure," he replies. "For one minute of your time, I would share you with a thousand other men."

I laugh. "Well, let's not overestimate my abilities here."

He grins at me. "I would never underestimate you, *mi tesoro*. I like being with you. But I'm a wounded animal these days. It's probably best that you not depend entirely on me."

The Volvo stops in front of my apartment building. I caress his jaw then kiss him. "You're going to be fine, *Profe*. And I would love to have a next time with you."

Tomás smiles, and it's so warm, my heart melts. "Until next

time then, Helena." I kiss him again, and it starts to get hot and heavy. He groans and pulls back. "Go, go! Or we are never getting out of this car."

"Much as I like that idea, I'm all worn out. You have a wonderful night, Tomás," I say and step out of the car.

Tomás waits until I'm inside the apartment building before putting the car in gear. I wave to him as he drives away.

Then I note an Otsego police car parked beside the building. "What the hell?" My chest tightens. Jack's not here, is he?

I remind myself I live in a secure building and go up to my apartment. I'm just putting my keys in the lock when McKenzy throws the door open. "I am so sorry," she whispers. "But there's still time to make a run for it!"

"I wouldn't try it." I hear Jack's voice and slowly poke my head in the door to see him sitting in the living room. With my parents—and Melody.

Fuck.

"How did they even get in here?" I hiss to McKenzy.

She hangs her head. "Officer Collins said if I didn't let them in, they'd wait outside until you were done with your date, and then he'd haul you out of the car in front of God and everyone."

"Well, there's an unsurprising abuse of power," I mutter. I squeeze McKenzy's shoulder. "It's okay. I can handle this."

"*We* can handle this," McKenzy corrects firmly, reminding me of why she's my best friend.

I step fully through the door in probably the most trampy thing any of them have ever seen me wear. My mother lets out a gasp. My father grunts disapprovingly. Melody, who is currently wearing something about as revealing as I am—which is conservative for her—grins triumphantly while letting out a "Tsk."

Jack balls his hands into fists on the arms of the chair he's sitting in. "Nice dress," he growls.

"Thanks. I was on a date," I reply sweetly, knowing it'll piss him off. He wasn't so happy when I broke up with him.

"Clearly," Jack seethes.

"You wore *that* trampy thing out in public?!" my mother yelps.

I walk to the center of the living room so the seated members of my family and Jack are surrounding me. If I'm being called into some sort of intervention, I'm at least going to do it properly. I do a little twirl for them all. "I had to out-do someone's soon-to-be-ex-wife. I think I did okay."

"Y-You were out with a married man?" My mother twists some tissue in her hands, then dabs at her mascara. Clearly, she's been distraught over me.

"I was," I respond, folding my arms over my chest. "The divorce is almost final. Not that it's any of your business."

"Harper, for shame." Melody lays it on thick. "And Jack tells us he was your former college professor too. That's pretty slutty."

I scowl at her.

"Remind me, is it two or three married men you've home wrecked now?" McKenzy asks her.

"We're not discussing Melody," my father inserts. "We're discussing you, Harper. How could you shame us this way?"

"Well, first of all, I'd love to know how Jack's getting all his information. I'm sure his sergeant would too," I say sweetly, shooting Jack a withering glare. "Second of all, you don't get to control my life. You're the ones who said I needed to find a way to make money, or you'd bring me home to Otsego. I'm not going back there. I'd rather sleep on a park bench."

My mother sniffles, pressing the fraying tissue to her nose.

"This is not the way we raised you, young lady," my father snaps. "If I knew you'd be whoring around, I'd have sent money."

"You'll be happy to know I don't need it anymore. Damien took care of that," I counter proudly. "Well, Damien and Rafe, but Damien made sure I'd never have to go on another app date again. People are interested in my art."

My father snorts. "Who cares about your little hobby? Honestly, come home and take that dispatcher job Jack worked out for you. Stop this nonsense."

"Oh, great, so my controlling ex-boyfriend can keep tabs on me all the time? Pass." Tears sting my eyes. *Hobby. That's right, my whole life's work is just a 'hobby' to them.*

"Jack is a nice boy!" my mother argues. "You just don't appreciate being taken care of by a good man."

"As evidenced by his keeping tabs on my every movement even though we haven't been dating in over a year," I reply. A bad feeling creeps up my spine. I was just using that point for effect but... has he really been keeping tabs on me? He knew about my date with Tomás...

I glare at Melody. Maybe it was her feeding him information, trying to rile him up.

"That's really creepy," McKenzy adds. I'm glad I have her in my corner.

"It's sweet," my mother retorts. "Every girl should have a man who cares that much about her."

I wish, just for that moment, I still had the wrist and arm bruises to show her how much he 'cares' about me. "Look, you're all here to make me feel ashamed of my life choices. I don't. Why don't you go home and pray for me or whatever it is you're going to do?"

"Four men is a 'lifestyle' now?" Jack asks blandly.

"FOUR MEN?" my mother and father shout together. My mother looks as though she may faint.

Melody lets out a low whistle. "That beats my record."

"Doubt it," McKenzy sneers.

I pat McKenzy's hand. "She's not worth it. Even my parents think she's a lost cause."

Melody looks affronted. "You...!"

"No daughter of mine is going to date four men at once! And one of them married to boot!" my father roars.

In that moment, under all their disapproving glares, I make a decision. "I guess I'm no daughter of yours then," I whisper.

FIFTEEN

Disowned and Dismissed

Harper

My mother gasps. "What are you saying?"

"I'm saying get out of my apartment," I state clearly.

"Yeah, get out!" McKenzy backs me up.

"I swear, young lady, the moment we step foot out that door, you can consider yourself officially disowned," my father snaps, rising and tugging my mother up with him. "You're going against decency, and I will not have that in my house!"

"This isn't your house," I remind him. "And you go ahead and take that up with your preacher or whoever. I'm completely at peace with my decision."

Melody stands and puts her arms around my parents. "I'm so sorry this turned out so horribly. I'd hope to help you intervene."

"You're the biggest whore I've ever met," McKenzy says snarkily.

"Melody has repented," my father says. "As should you, Harper."

"Oh, is that sixteen or seventeen times now?" McKenzy replies, ticking them off on her fingers. "There was that first time after Vegas when she was fifteen…."

I put a hand over McKenzy's mouth. I don't need to hear any more. "You'd better get out now while the getting is good," I tell everyone else.

My father pales. My mother leans on him for strength, still dabbing her eyes.

Melody is maniacally happy. I can see it in her eyes. "Repent," she says with fake sadness. "Or you'll never be able to go home."

"Gee, and I was so looking forward to it." I fight my roiling feelings with angry sarcasm.

My mother shakes her head as they make their way to the door. "Who are you?" she chokes before my father puts his arms around her and Melody and escorts them out.

"That wasn't very smart, Harper," Jack sighs.

Ah, yes. That asshole's still here.

"I don't remember asking for your opinion." I turn to him. "You can leave too."

"What if I don't want to?" he replies, a hint of danger in his tone.

McKenzy grabs my arm. I can tell by the way her fingers tremble that she's scared. "She said to leave. Hurry up before we call the cops."

Jack raises an eyebrow at us and gestures to his full police uniform. It doesn't escape me that he has a gun on his hip. "I am the police."

"Not in St. Paul, you're not," I remind him, standing my ground.

"Harper, you're sweet, but don't push it. You know what happens when I get angry," he says, rising.

I swallow. Shit, shit, *shit*, shit, shit!

"I told you to leave," I repeat.

"She told you to leave," McKenzy echoes. She's still standing just behind me, holding onto my arm for fortitude.

Hell, if I had someone in front of me, I'd be clinging to them too. I wish I did. I don't like the idea of there being nothing between me and an angry Jack.

"I think you should invite me to dinner," he adds instead of going. "I think we have a lot to talk about."

McKenzy can't be here for this. I need her to leave. I need her to leave so she doesn't get hurt. "McKenzy, you should go. Jack and I need to talk."

"There's a good girl." He smirks. "McKenzy, if you call the police, I will make sure you are both arrested for drug possession." He reaches into his vest and pulls out a baggie with some sort of white substance in it. "Trust me, it'll stick."

She grips my arm harder, tugging me backward with her. "I think we should both leave," she says, her voice quavering.

"Let's see here…where to stash the cocaine…" Jack murmurs, looking around.

Fuck.

"I'll stay. You go, McKenzy," I tell her, prying her hand off my arm and giving her a gentle push toward the door. "It'll be okay. We're just going to talk."

"I don't believe you," she whispers.

I wince at being caught in my own lie. "Please?" I beg.

She looks at Jack and shakes her fist. "You'd better not hurt her again!"

"I'd get out while the getting's good, McKenzy," Jack growls.

With one last look at me, my best friend turns and runs from the apartment.

Now, I'm all alone with Jack.

* * *

Rafe

An insistent beeping wakes me up. I glance at my phone. It's past midnight on a game night. Who the fuck needs me this late?

McKenzy Jasper: Rafe! Help!

McKenzy Jasper: Help!

McKenzy Jasper: It's an emergency!

I frown. McKenzy, as I recall, once threatened to pickle my dick for what she thought I'd done to Harper. I didn't even know she still had my number. Why does she need help now?

Rafe Maloney: What?

McKenzy Jasper: I'm outside our apartment! Jack's in there! He's going to hurt Harper!

That wakes me right up.

Rafe Maloney: I'm on my way. Text more details while I'm in the car and be there to let me in the security door.

I jump out of bed, throw on whatever I grab off a chair, and run down to the parking garage. *Who's Jack? Why is he in Harper's apartment? What does McKenzy mean he's going to hurt her?*

McKenzy doesn't disappoint. My car reads her text messages to me while I peel out of the parking garage and away from my downtown Minneapolis apartment building. I don't really care if I get a ticket as long as I lead a high-speed chase of cops to Harper's apartment.

McKenzy Jasper: Jack's an Otsego cop. They used to date. Broke up over a year ago. But her parents brought him here tonight for some weird intervention about her dating life, and now he's threatening her! She made me leave, but I'm sticking by the door and recording this shit if he puts his hands on her!

I do talk-to-text to reply.

Rafe Maloney: Twenty minutes. Fuck, he's a cop?

McKenzy Jasper: He said he was going to get us for drug possession if we don't do what he says.

I groan and get on the highway, pressing the gas pedal as far as it will go.

Rafe Maloney: I'll let you know when I'm at the building. You still have to let me in, McKenzy, don't forget!

McKenzy Jasper: I can do that from my phone. This is the 21st century.

Rafe Maloney: Good. And McKenzy?

McKenzy Jasper: Yeah?

Rafe Maloney: Be careful.

Honestly, where are the fucking cops to pull you over when you need one? I don't run into one on my way to Carleton Artist Lofts. I park the Corvette in front of the resident entrance and text McKenzy to let me in.

The door buzzes just as I grab the handle.

I take the stairs two at a time and see McKenzy cowering beside her apartment door. I can hear shouting inside.

"Stay here," I order her. She just nods.

I slam the door open and take in the scene before me. Jack, in full police uniform—with a gun—is standing over Harper, who looks terrified.

Yep. It's official. I'm gonna become a cop-killer tonight. "Just what the *fuck* do you think you're doing?" I roar at Jack.

McKenzy, against my wishes, comes in behind me, and God bless her, starts filming the whole thing. "Speak up, Officer Collins. The Internet wants to hear why you're in here with your gun drawn on Harper."

Jack goes pale. "Rafe Maloney? What are you doing here?"

"Finding out if pigs fly if you don't get the *fuck* out of here right now!" I yell.

He looks down at Harper, looks at me, looks at McKenzy with her phone pointed at him, and looks at me again. "Should have taken her fucking phone," he mutters. He steps around Harper like she's trash and walks past me, giving me a wide berth.

The coward isn't so scared of McKenzy though. He grabs her phone and throws it. It shatters on the floor. "If that video survived the fall, you don't want to know what will happen to you if you post it," he threatens her.

I round on him and punch him so hard in the face that I hear a crack. I can only hope it's not the bones of my throwing hand.

Jack stumbles back, holding his eye. "You… you son of a bitch!" He fumbles for the strap over his gun and unsnaps it.

"I'd think twice" Harper says from the floor, and there's my girl holding her phone and recording him.

He quickly snaps the strap back down. "I hope you get your asses whipped tomorrow," he says, and hurries out of the apartment.

"Fucking asshole," I grunt, just starting to feel a throbbing in my knuckles.

Harper struggles up, and I forget my knuckles, going to her side. "Sugar, are you okay?"

She's shaking, and her arm is bruised, so I'm instantly sorry I didn't pummel that bastard until every bone in his body shattered. I wrap my arms around her and hug her tightly. She starts to cry, hugging me back.

"It's okay. He's gone now. He's not coming back," I assure her. "Yo, McKenzy, you okay? I'll replace your phone. You've got big, round hairy ones, both of you."

"Uh… I think that's a compliment," McKenzy says. She kicks the shards of her phone aside and goes into the kitchen, pulling out two bags of frozen veggies from the freezer and wrapping them in two different towels.

"Sugar, your arm is hurt," I inform Harper once McKenzy hands me both wrapped bags. I guide Harper to the couch and sit her down, settling next to her so I can hold the towel-wrapped freezer veggies to her arm.

"Rafe, your knuckles," she groans, taking my bruised hand. Lucky for me, it is just a little scuffed, which means that crunch must have been Jack's bones and not mine. *Vikings quarterback for the win!*

A sharp pain brings me out of my mental victory dance, and I see Harper is laying vegetables on my hand while I'm holding vegetables to her lip. We look at each other and start laughing.

"I'm just going to go to my bedroom. Harper has a queen, so I think you two will be comfy-cozy." McKenzy smiles. She sweeps up what used to be her phone and dumps it in the trash, double checking she locked the door after Jack left, then heads off to her room.

I pull the vegetables away from Harper's arm to survey the damage. "Guess we won't be doing much then."

She kisses my knuckles, and involuntarily, I wince. "Not too much hand-holding or heavy petting anyway."

"I have two hands," I protest. "Though, just so we're clear, we're having sex in your room, right?"

"As long as… you don't mind… um… I…" she stutters.

It's so cute. I boop her on the nose. "Are you saying sex in the shower might be in order?"

"Yes," she says with relief.

"No problem, sugar." I get up, toss the vegetables and towels on the coffee table, then lift her in my arms.

"Rafe, we might want to eat those!" she objects.

"I'll buy you some news," I insist.

She blushes and loops her arms around my neck. "Oh. Okay." I carry her to the bathroom. "Rafe?"

"Yes?"

She presses her lips to mine in a very soft kiss. "Thank you for coming."

"Hey, sugar. I'm always gonna be there for you. Always," I whisper back.

SIXTEEN

Coming for Me

Harper

Water streams down my body as Rafe soaps me up, his hard length pressing into my back. I worry about the state of his hand, but he's not complaining, so I decide not to say anything.

He's treating me so gently and doing everything from washing my hair to washing my legs and even up between them. I lean back against him, one arm going up around his neck, the other gripping his thigh as he starts fingering me. I'm still tired from Tomás, but it still feels so deliciously good.

"Guess I'm going to have to be gentle with my sugar," Rafe murmurs, kissing my shoulder. "Wild night?"

"Kinda, yeah." My cheeks flush.

He strokes my cheek. "Don't be embarrassed. I'm glad you had fun, and someone's got you nice and loosened up for me, so, bonus."

I laugh. "Glad I could make your night."

"Well, you haven't yet. But you're about to." Rafe takes my hands and kisses my fingers one at a time, then leans me forward and presses my hands against the shower wall.

Instinctively, I brace myself as he guides himself to my entrance then pushes just the tip inside. I glance back at him, and he gives me another inch, sliding in very slowly and sweetly. "Rafe…"

"I know you're tired, sugar. We'll go nice and slow," he says.

Our breathing merges, and he starts kissing his way down my back, as far as he can get without pulling out. He kisses me everywhere he can reach, rocking his hips slightly so he's thrusting just an inch in and out of me. I turn to face him, and he lifts me up. He buries his face in my neck and then pushes all the way inside of me. "I love you, Rafe," I say softly, curling my fingers into his hair.

"I love you too, Harper." Rafe's voice cracks. He starts making love to me in earnest, and I cling to him as he thrusts. One arm holds me against him, while the other sweeps over my breasts, then down to my clit.

When I come, I cry out his name.

"Ahh, sugar…" Rafe groans as he grunts a few times and then releases.

We end up having to wash again, of course, but this time I get to wash Rafe too, so I don't mind one bit. His body is so beautiful, and I get to touch it.

He's being so gentle, I can hardly believe this is the man I thought would cheat on me. Then the dam bursts as all the fear from being at Jack's mercy finally breaks free. I choke on a sob.

"I'm so glad you're okay," he whispers over and over. "I'm sorry I didn't get here sooner, but I'm glad you're okay. Oh, Harper." He wraps his arms around me and presses his cheek against my shoulder. His cheek is rough with a five o'clock shadow, but I don't care. All I know is he's holding me, and everything is okay now because he's here.

We stay like that for a long time. We're cocooned there in that moment in a way that reality can't touch. It's still so overwhelming, I don't know what to think.

He pulls me even harder against him so I'm plastered to his muscular body, the cascading water relaxing both of us. Eventually, we get out of the shower and start drying off.

"You do know I'm staying the night, right, sugar?" he asks me.

"I kind of figured," I replied. "But… don't you have a game tomorrow?"

"I do, but it's not until the afternoon" he says. "I'll be fine, assuming my hand is okay."

Shit.

"I'm sorry, Rafe," I sigh.

He wraps me, naked, in his arms. "It's fine. If it meant saving you from that asshole, it's worth it, even if I can't play."

"I don't think your coach is going to see it that way if you can't," I mumble against his pec.

"I'll explain the situation," he replies. "Oh, speaking of which…" He grabs his phone off the vanity and shoots off a text. "I'm just letting them know I'll need to have it looked at before the game."

"Oh, God, it's the Vikings-Packers game, isn't it?" I remember as his phone almost immediately starts blowing up.

Rafe picks up his phone, answers a few texts from his teammates, I assume, and shrugs. "Yes, but our backup quarterback is good this year. If I can't go, we'll still beat them." He kisses me gently. "There's only one of you."

I smile at him, my eyes swimming with tears. "You say the sweetest things."

"I love you," he says again.

"I love you, too. Let's go to bed."

* * *

EVEN THOUGH HIS phone is vibrating so much it can't be set down for fear it'll jump right off whatever surface and shatter on the floor, Rafe is adamant about staying the night with me. The next morning, McKenzy is more than happy to make him eggs and bacon for breakfast, but when we're done eating, she looks at me.

"Rafe," I try. "You can't stay here forever. Your coach is going to have your head, and you need to get your hand looked at."

"I didn't break anything." He looks petulant. "I don't want that asshole coming back around here."

"Last time, I let him in because he was with Harper's parents," McKenzy explains. "I won't let him in again. He can't get past the security door."

"But…" he argues.

"Someone is going to steal your Corvette if they haven't already," I warn him.

That gives him pause, then he shakes his head. "Fuck the Corvette. It's probably missing its tires and its stereo by now."

Privately, I agree with him. We aren't exactly in a rough neighborhood, but this isn't Corvette territory either. "If it is, I'm sorry about that too."

He leans over and kisses me as we sit together on the couch. "Stop apologizing. I don't care about the car as much as I care about you."

"Ra-afe," I sigh. "You need to go. I want your team doctor or whatever you have, to make sure your hand is okay before the game."

His phone tries to vibrate itself off the coffee table, but he catches it before it falls. "Fine, fine. If you're really sure he can't get back in."

"He can't," I confirm.

Rafe finally answers his phone. "Yeah, Coach. Sorry, I had to mix it up last night with some asshole who was beating on my girlfriend. I hit him with my throwing hand."

He holds the phone away from his ear as the coach begins spewing profanities. "I'm coming in. I just needed to make sure he wasn't coming back. No, I don't think anything's broken. Yes, my girl's safe now." With a sigh, he hangs up the phone. "If the Corvette is wrecked, I'll call a cab. You call or text me the second he shows up again, yeah?"

"I will," I promise. "But hopefully you scared him off."

Rafe's eyebrows draw together in a distant, troubled expression. "Guys like him aren't always so easily scared off." He shakes his head, and his smile returns. "Love you, sugar." He kisses me and slowly leaves the apartment, waving at me before he walks out. McKenzy locks the door behind him.

"You have a star football player, a billionaire, a hot Spanish professor, and a farm boy who makes you laugh all chasing after you." McKenzy chuckles. "You have got to be the luckiest girl in the world. Except for Jack the jackass, of course."

"You've given him a new nickname, have you?" I grin.

"Nickname? Who says it's a nickname?" she shoots back.

We laugh together. Then I remember my farm-boy-who-makes-me-laugh. We have a date scheduled for today. "Shoot, what time is it? I'm supposed to be out at Scott's farm at four!"

"Keep your pants on, it's only ten, and it only takes like forty minutes to get there," she replies. "You're telling him about the others today, aren't you?"

"First thing," I confirm. "I don't want there to be any misunderstandings between anyone and, well, anyone."

McKenzy grabs my arm, pulling me to my feet. "Come on. We need to check the closets."

"Closets? For what?" I ask.

"For the perfect I'm-dating-three-other-guys-but-still-like-you-and-aren't-I-sexy-enough-to-share outfit." She starts rummaging through my closet, makes a face, and closes the door. "Remind me to take you shopping." She then drags me into her room, which is an explosion of clothes, shoes, and purses, which makes my brain scream.

She goes to her bursting closet, diving deep, then comes up with a yellow sundress with little daisies embroidered all over it. "This. This is definitely it!"

"It always amazes me that your clothes don't get wrinkled, even when they're shoved in there and tossed around the room," I say in bemusement.

McKenzy grins at me. "It's a gift. Now go try it on! I'll find some white sandals to go with it. I'll even make sure they're flats this time. You're going to a farm, after all."

"Thanks." I chuckle and do some more painting before I start getting ready.

Hours later, when I go downstairs, I look around for Jack's car, but I don't see anything. I look at the car I share with McKenzy.

Would Jack know which one it is? Could he have done something to it? My nerves are shot, even though I know I can take an Uber out to Vermillion. I just don't want to feel violated like that.

Luckily, when I start it up, the car is just fine. I start out of the parking lot. A tan Ford sedan is waiting, parked along the street outside the parking lot. My chest seizes. *Oh, God, it's him!*

I don't dare stop now. I look in my rearview mirror, trying to see his license plate so maybe I can call the St. Paul police while I'm driving, but the plate is covered in dirt. It seems a bit strategic to me.

With no other alternative in mind, I decide to simply drive out to Vermillion with the Ford on my tail. Once I get to the farm, Scott will be there.

After I get on the highway, I'm about to call Rafe, as I promised, but the Ford swerves around me and pulls ahead. Its windows are so tinted that I can't see who's inside. But since they aren't following me anymore....

Maybe it's just a coincidence? I put my phone down. Our Honda is too old to have Bluetooth, and my hands are too shaky for me to safely dial while driving..

I'm jumpy all the way to Scott's farm. Something just doesn't feel right.

I arrive at the farm at 3:57 PM, still shaky but alive and not being tailed by Jack. I consider this a win. The long, gravel driveway stops in front of the house and opens into a wide patch in front of the barn.

Turning off the car, I start for the house. I knock and ring the doorbell, but no one answers.

Oh, shit, did Jack get here first? Has he done something to Scott? I panic and whip around in a circle, looking for some sign of Scott.

A scraping and thumping sound comes from the barn.

I run there, startling the cows as I enter. They moo angrily at me. I don't care.

"Scott?" I call. "Scott?!"

Another scraping sound. Then something falls from the barn ceiling into one of the stalls.

I scream.

SEVENTEEN

The Barn

Harper

"Harper?" I hear Scott call from above me.

A cow meanders over to the hay that just fell and begins to munch on it, giving me a glare. The others are very agitated, stomping their feet and mooing in various states from anger to fear.

"Scott?" I croak.

He comes down a ladder, shirtless, wearing only a pair of Wranglers. He's sweaty, his chestnut hair plastered to his forehead. "What's wrong? What's the screaming about? Are you okay?"

I run to him, and completely ignoring the fact that he's drenched in sweat, launch myself into his arms, hugging him hard. "Oh, thank God. No, everything is okay. I just couldn't find you."

He wraps his arms around me and drops his chin onto the top of my head. "Something's wrong. I know you well enough to hear it in your voice, Harper."

"I thought someone might have hurt you," I confess into his chest.

"Hurt me?" He sounds confused, and I don't blame him. "Who would hurt me?"

"My ex-boyfriend is back. He's stalking me. At least, I think he's stalking me. I don't know." I look up at him. "I was afraid maybe he got here before me, and… I don't know. I don't know what I was thinking."

His eyes narrow, and I know he's seen the bruises on my arm. He touches my arm just beneath the purple mark. "Did he do this to you?"

"Yes," I admit softly. I hate it, but my eyes are welling up with tears again. "It's a long story. A really long story. I mean, kind of a short story, but there's stuff I need to tell you in the middle, so kind of a long story too."

"Okay." He glances at the cows. "Give me one second. I need to calm them down. As long as you're okay? I meant to do this earlier, but I had to help deliver a calf at my neighbor's and I got behind."

"I'm okay," I assure him.

It takes about fifteen minutes—fifteen minutes where I'm ready to burst with my information—but Scott finally calms the cows down.

"Now," he says, returning to me. "Let's go to the house and talk, okay?"

I glance at the barn door, then at the house, then back at Scott. My whole body is trembling.

"Or not," he amends quickly. He looks at the ladder to the hayloft then guides me over to it. "At least you're wearing decent shoes for a farm today. Sort of. They still don't look like they've seen a lot of dirt."

I start climbing the ladder, grateful we're not leaving the barn. "I don't know what's happening to me. I just have this bad feeling. I'm sorry."

"Hey, I get to show you more of the farm this way," he replies kindly.

Once we're in the hayloft, Scott brings me over to some hay bales where we sit down. "Okay, tell me what's happened," he requests, taking my hands.

"Well, over a year ago I was dating this cop…" I begin. Then I shake my head. "No, I need to start somewhere else. I've been…

uh…seeing a few other people…" I swallow, looking at our joined hands. Scott has not let go. I take this as a good sign. "Like, three. I wasn't seeing them when we met, but they contacted me through the app… and it just sort of snowballed from there. I don't want to stop seeing you, but I don't want to stop seeing them either. Make sense?"

He squeezes my hands. "Makes sense."

I look up. His eyes are kind and understanding, and he still hasn't let me go. "Okay, so, is it all right with you that I'm seeing other people too?"

"Yes." Scott nods. "Organic farmer, remember? I know a lot about animals. If bulls get to have more than one cow, why not the other way around?" He blushes. "Or something less offensive than that."

Overjoyed, I kiss him. "I wanted to tell you to your face. That's why I didn't text it to you."

"I like that and that you had the courage to tell me." He frowns. "Now, about this ex-boyfriend cop…"

"Jack Collins. He's a cop in Otsego. That's where I'm from, where my parents live." I bite my lip. "He was nice in the beginning, but then he got controlling, and he'd grab me and leave bruises, as you can see. I broke up with him, but, well… my parents decided they liked him, so they brought him to this intervention…" I explained all about the intervention, which led to explaining about Melody, which led to explaining about Rafe. "So, McKenzy still had Rafe's number from before, so she texted him after Jack and I told her to get out and—"

"Well, we have to fix that," Scott interrupts me.

I frown, confused. "Fix what?"

"McKenzy should have my number. Hell, she should have the number of all the guys you're dating right now. I'm sure we'd all like to show up at times like that," he responds.

"Oh." I hadn't thought about that. "Good point."

Scott strokes my hair. "And that's when he hurt you?"

"Yeah."

"Has he ever hit you before?" he asks.

I shake my head. "No. Just the grabbing and the bruising, and he shook me once but... he hasn't hit me. Yet.

"It sucks he's a policeman. Otherwise, you could report him and not end up bringing down trouble on your head." He sighs.

"That's exactly what I was thinking," I reply. "I mean, I could still go report him, but I don't want his cop buddies up my ass too."

Scott tucks me into him. I can smell sweet hay, sweat, cow, and all kinds of other comforting farm smells. "On the one hand, if you don't report him, they don't have this incident to refer back to if he does something else. But if you do report him, he'll probably escalate and do something worse. This is a bad position to be in, but I'm here for you, okay?"

"Okay." I let out a long breath. "Scott?"

"Hmm?"

"Tell me something funny," I say.

He smiles at me. "I'm just thinking about Rafe."

"Rafe?" I retort, wrinkling my nose. "Why are you thinking about Rafe?"

"The Vikings-Packers game of course! He'd better get it together because I've got him on my Fantasy Football roster." He chuckles indignantly.

I can't help myself. I laugh until I cry.

"Harper, it's going to be okay." Scott holds me until the tears subside.

Then I kiss him.

He deepens the kiss, and I can taste my tears on his tongue. He leans me back and we tumble into the hay. That sweet smell fills my nose, as well as the masculine scent that is entirely Scott.

"Is this okay?" he asks me, his hand sliding under my dress and up my thigh. "I don't want to take advantage."

"This is great," I reply. "Let's keep going. I've missed you."

"I've missed you too," he murmurs. I run my hands over his sweaty body, his firm, work-hardened muscles a playground for my fingertips.

Scott toes off his boots and shucks his jeans completely, and I find he's gone commando. He's naked, hard, and still has one of the biggest dicks I've ever seen.

"Harper." He kisses me again while pulling my panties down my legs, over my sandals, and tossing them aside. I wonder if we'll ever find them again in all the hay. Then I don't wonder anything at all because his fingers have found me where I ache the most.

"Oh, God," I moan as his fingers enter me, rubbing my clit with his thumb. "Oh, Scott."

"That's it, darlin'," he assures me, his breath feathering my ear. "You're so wet, but I want to make sure you're ready for me."

I whimper and wrap my arms around his neck. His other hand sweeps one side of my dress down over my shoulder, exposing my breast to him. I hadn't felt a need for a bra, given the formed empire waist of the sundress, and the sound he makes in his throat tells me that it was a good choice. He latches onto my nipple, rolling it with his tongue while he continues to pleasure me with his fingers.

His cock is hard against my thigh, dribbling a little bit onto my skin. The ravenous way he wants me just turns me on even more, and I cry out as my orgasm crests over me, slamming into me like a great wave.

While I'm still riding my high, Scott removes his fingers and pushes his big dick into me. *All* the way in. It feels so good, I have to keep my eyes closed as my head tips back in ecstasy.

"Harper," he groans and starts to thrust faster. I cling to him, not even aware of what a mess he's making of me. His fingers tangle my hair. His mouth leaves wet kisses over my breast and skin. My lips swell because of the hungry way he kisses me. I don't give a damn about any of it, about the mess, about being half-in my clothes, about the hay scratching my legs. I just want him to ride me until I can't stand it anymore.

We come together, crying out, gripping each other tightly as though that can prolong the moment. Afterward, we shiver even though we aren't cold, his dick still buried inside me.

"I had a picnic planned, but do you want to go again first?" Scott asks after he catches his breath.

"Oh, yes, please," I all but beg, rolling my hips against his.

EIGHTEEN

The Stalker

Harper

I never knew how insatiable farm boys were—in more ways than one—until I met Scott. His stomach is a bottomless pit while we eat, but that makes me more comfortable in a way. I don't feel like I have to pick and peck at my food like a little bird.

After the picnic under an apple tree, we went inside and had sex again on his sofa, which ended with us laughing in a tangle of limbs on the floor. We then went to the bedroom and, after an hour or so, had sex again.

By the time I think I should be getting home, I'm tired, and the sun is starting to set. "This is your fault," I tell him as he helps me to my car, one of my arms slung over his shoulders.

"Not sorry," he chuckles.

I give him a tired swat. "You know I'll be pulling hay out of my hair for a week, right?"

"That'll just give you enough time to come back here and scoop up some more." He is completely unrepentant. I like it.

I slide into my car, wincing a little. I have really been giving my body a workout these last few days. Not that I regret a minute of it.

"I'll see you Thursday?" I ask, confirming our agreed-upon next date.

"You'll see me Thursday," he replies, grinning from ear to ear. He gives me a swift kiss, then puts my seatbelt on me, and closes the car door. He taps his fingers on the roof of the car. "Drive safe."

"I will." I wait for him to get back to his porch then begin driving down the gravel driveway toward the main road.

When I round the bend and can see past the trees, I note that tan Ford sedan parked across the front of the driveway.

My breath catches, and I stop the car a good thirty feet shy of Jack, who is getting out of the sedan with the dark-tinted windows. He glowers at me, a look so dangerous in his eyes that I immediately hit reverse and speed back down the driveway, backward.

* * *

SCOTT

I'm just going back into the house when the little Honda Harper drives comes careening back down the gravel driveway. Backward. She spins in a complete one-eighty in the open area between the house and the barn, nearly hitting both, then parks the car in front of the barn doors—sideways—and jumps out, leaving the car running.

She's paler than fresh milk. I jump down off the porch and run to her, just as a tan Ford skids toward me. By the way he's driving, I'm pretty sure whoever is driving—and you can't tell because of the window tint—really means to hit me.

"Scott!" Harper screams.

I dive out of the way, behind her car, and the Ford stops just shy of the bumper. I don't think I could pass a dollar between the two, but he doesn't hit it.

The door of the Ford swings open, and I see a man with a crew cut step out. He's not in uniform, but I'm guessing this is Harper's ex.

"You nearly hit me there asshole," I say, glaring at him as I stand. I'm grateful I didn't send Harper off just in my boxers or something. I am fully clothed and just about as pissed off as I can get. I plan to use this to my advantage.

Jack—and I'm sure it's Jack—spits on the ground at my feet. "Have you been messing around with my girl?" he asks, his voice tight with anger.

I stick my hand in my pocket. "Well, damn, sir. I don't know anything about *your* girl. Are you talking about Harper?"

He grabs me by the shirtfront. "Yes, you goddamn hick, I'm talking about Harper."

"Well, see, I guess that's where we have a difference of opinion," I drawl. "I think Harper's my girl. Should we ask her?"

Jack winds back and punches me.

"Jack!" Harper cries. "Stop it! Stop!"

I'm a farm boy from a small town. I've been hit before and done some hitting. I guess it's time to do some hitting. I spit blood, thinking I must now have a split lip. It's Harper's bruised arm that has me shoving Jack off me and hitting him with a set of good one-two punches. That asshole's too city to even know what hit him.

"You know you just hit a cop, right?" he snarls at me, wiping at a bloody nose. Looks like I broke it. Good.

"Yep, but I don't really give a damn" I reply.

Jack reaches behind his back, and I get a bad feeling. My feeling is confirmed when he whips out a revolver. "I could shoot you right now, and everyone would say it was self-defense."

"I wouldn't," Harper says.

We both look to the side and see her filming the whole thing with her phone.

Jack goes a shade of purple I haven't even seen on an eggplant and points a threatening finger in her direction. "You knock that off right now. I'll get to you later."

"No." She's so brave, I want to kiss her. Almost as much as I want to knock this guy around until I get some sense through his thick skull.

When he starts her way, I grab him in a headlock from behind. He growls at me and tries to get free, but I guess they don't make city cops as tough as farm boys because whatever he does, it doesn't get the image of Harper's arm out of my head, and as long as that's on my mind, I can hang on until his damn neck breaks if I have to.

He finally calms down enough that I can let him go then tries to take a potshot at me. But I see it coming, so I just sidestep his swing.

"Are you done yet?" I ask as Harper continues to film us.

"You keep your filthy hands off her, you son of a bitch." He points at me. "Or I'm coming back here with reinforcements, and I will burn your farm to the ground!"

"Can you face the camera when you say that? I want to make sure every person on the jury can read that without any problems," Harper chimes in.

Jack jumps as though he's forgotten she was even there.

"She's so thoughtful that way," I add.

He finally looks at her phone with the amount of trepidation his situation deserves. He knows he's screwed.

"I'll be back, you fucking backwoods hick," he grunts, putting his finger in my face now.

I give him a different finger.

Jack chokes on his rage but glances at the phone again then stomps over to his car. "You're both going to be sorry."

"Just go," Harper says.

He gets in his car and peels away, spraying gravel everywhere.

I go over to Harper. Her phone is shaking in her hand. I take it from her and stop the recording then just manage to catch her before she sinks to the ground on wobbly legs. "Whoa there. It's okay. He's gone. I'm here. We're just going to get you back to the house so you can sit down."

"He'll be back," Harper whispers, trembling in my arms.

"So he says. I think it's time we call everyone in," I tell her, making a split-second decision.

"Who's everyone?" she asks, blinking at me. I'm not sure she even has the capacity to focus right now.

I hug her to me. "Your other three guys. Seems we're all in danger, and I know we all care that you are too. Is Rafe the only other one who knows your ex is stalking you?"

"It… it wasn't an issue with the other two. I thought. Oh, God,

I remember seeing an Otsego squad car one day, and that stupid Ford has been everywhere.... He... knows about all of you," she stutters. "He talked about it in front of my parents. Oh, God..."

"Take some deep breaths. Here, you hold onto your phone." I hand it to her, and she holds it against her chest like a security blanket. Then I scoop her up in my arms. "We're just going to head into the house, and you're going to sit down. Hell, maybe even lie down. If you tell me who they are on your phone, I'll call them."

Harper shakes her head. "It's my responsibility. I should call them."

"Harper," I respond sternly. "Your teeth are chattering. You need to let me take care of this, okay?"

I know she wants to fight me on it, but when I get her lying on the sofa with a pillow under her head, she finally gives in. "Okay."

"Okay." I take off her sandals, then hold out my hand for her phone. "Names?"

Harper unlocks it and hands it to me. "Rafe Maloney. Tomás García del Rio, and Damien Blackwood."

I stare at her. "Damien fucking Blackwood?"

She blushes. "Yeah."

"Jesus. How am I supposed to compete with him?" I groan, but grin at her so she knows I'm kidding.

"You can compete with him," she teases back.

I raise an eyebrow. "Really?"

"Really." And I know she's being honest.

Then I somber up, and all I want to do in this world is protect her..

NINETEEN

Team Harper

Harper

Damien is the last to arrive, late in the evening, but then, he flew in from New York. He's still in his power suit and, since Scott warned him over the phone about Jack, he has two bodyguards with him.

Rafe, who is still on a high from the Viking's win earlier today, has made himself at home in one of Scott's armchairs, munching on some potato chips Scott had in the cupboard. He waves at Damien like they're old friends.

"Ah, yes. Thanks for padding my Fantasy Football score." Damien smiles as soon as he spots him.

"I told him the same thing," Scott says with a chuckle.

Rafe shrugs. "I do what I can."

Tomás leans against the wall, looking awkwardly at the others. I can't blame him, really. I mean, Forbes Top 50, Football Star, and we're all in Scott's house, so... yeah. But when he looks at me, there's determination in his eyes, and that makes my heart beat faster. He's not rich, he's not famous, and he's not trying to save the world through organic farming. But he does mold young minds, and he's good at it. I think that's really something.

"I assume we will be calling McKenzy and telling her to go stay with someone else for the time being?" Damien asks in a no-nonsense tone, immediately taking charge.

Rafe sits up and brushes crumbs off himself, instantly alert. I frown at him for getting crumbs on Scott's floor. "I'm going to send someone to take her to her parents'."

"Why is that necessary?" I ask. "It's a secure building—"

"He's a cop," all four say together. I suddenly feel like maybe we should've done something to warn McKenzy hours ago, but I still think the building is secure.

"He's a cop for now, anyway. He won't be in a week, if I have anything to do with it." Damien replies. "I hear there's a video?"

Scott hands him my unlocked phone. Damien plays the video, his frown deepening with every word that comes out of Jack's mouth. Actually, all of them are frowning by the end.

"I'm thinking he might be an apple short of a barrel," Scott suggests.

"He certainly needs a reality check," Rafe snorts. "Man, I wish I'd been there to hit him."

"Again?" I gape. "Rafe, that's your throwing hand!"

Rafe flexes his fingers, which still have small abrasions on the knuckles. "Worth it."

"Back to the matter at hand," Damien carries on. "I'm forwarding this to the Commissioner. Jack won't be able to dispense parking tickets by tomorrow."

"That will probably make him angry," Tomás points out quietly.

"And that's exactly why the girls won't be at the apartment until we can get a suitable protection detail set up," Damien replies. "But excellent point, Professor. García. Angry people are dangerous, true, but they also make mistakes. Like Jack did, allowing himself to be videotaped."

"Twice," Rafe adds. "But McKenzy's phone got shattered, so we don't have that one, unfortunately."

Damien nods. "This one is perfectly sufficient, I think. Now, about bodyguards…"

"I am happy to be with Harper when I don't have classes. If I need to, I'm sure I can take a leave of absence," Tomás begins.

"Good thinking. One of us should be with her as much as possible, but I'm going to hire professionals for both of them. We can each take shifts with Harper and report back to each other what is going on," Damien continues in a reasonable tone. "I'm assuming he knows where we all live. Therefore, I've decided to take Harper back to my penthouse tonight. I know she says her building is secure, but I have more than a buzzer system and hope in place to keep people out of my building."

"I'm right here," I grumble.

Scott pats my shoulder. "It's okay. We're just working out logistics."

"What if I say 'no'?" I ask testily.

All four heads turn my way.

"Are you planning to?" Damien finally responds.

I can imagine there's more he wants to say, probably something along the lines of 'I will take you back to my room and make you scream all night,' but the others have such equal expressions of horror on their faces that I just hunch my shoulders and say, "No."

I'm not a complete idiot after all. This Jack situation is serious.

"Good girl." Damien smirks and continues to the others. "So I'll take the first shift. Tomorrow, as long as everything is in place, we'll have the girls go back to their apartment. I was thinking perhaps Tomás could take tomorrow afternoon into evening. After your classes, of course. I took the liberty of checking your schedule."

Tomás blinks at him. "Oh. *Bueno.*"

"Rafe should go next. It will be after Monday Night Football after all, and several days before the Viking's next game. I'm not joking about my Fantasy Football line-up. I have a rather hefty bet going with one of my competitors, so you can't miss practice," Damien says.

"Far be it from me to screw up your points." Rafe grins.

"Precisely." Damien's expression is fearsome, and Rafe sobers.

"Yessir," Rafe coughs.

Scott rubs the back of my neck in a soothing motion as all these decisions are happening around me. He must know how annoyed I am. Touched–but annoyed.

"Any questions?" Damien concludes.

I raise my hand like I'm in school. "So, I'm going to your penthouse tonight. And tomorrow I can go back to my apartment? I wanted to get some pieces finished. *Someone* increased my popularity exponentially within the last couple of weeks, and now I have commission requests coming out of my eyeballs."

"If the security detail concludes that your apartment is unsafe, I will have your things moved to the penthouse. You can paint by the windows. Lots of natural light," Damien explains.

"Well, I mean, that's true, but… I'm one of those newfangled independent women your mother warned you about," I argue.

Damien bites back a smile. "I see. Well then, I suppose I'll just have to have Jack killed."

My jaw pops as it drops so hard. "Damien, no!"

"I don't think that asshole is worth the stain on your soul," Tomás says.

"I was joking. Sort of. I suppose he can live. For now," Damien muses, stroking his chin.

"Damien, really, listen to Tomás. He's not worth it," I plead.

Damien cracks a smile. "Don't worry, little red bird. I'll abstain. Well, I'll abstain from killing him. Other things…"

"TMI. TMI!" Rafe grumbles, making a time-out motion with his hands.

I chew my lip nervously. "I mean, I… we… uh… will probably…" I don't know how they will all react. It's one thing to tell them about each other separately. It's another thing to be smacked in the face with the truth of the situation when all four are in the same room.

"*Diviértete*." Tomás smiles.

"Yeah, what he said," Rafe agrees. "Have fun."

"And here I didn't think you were paying much attention in class, Rafael. But your test scores told a different story," Tomás says.

Rafe shrugs. "You were a great professor."

"*¿Bueno, ya estamos listos?*" Damien asks with a flawless accent.

"Yeah, I think we're done here. You and Harper go have great sex." Scott winks.

"Thank you. We plan to." Damien offers me his arm.

I just stare around at the four of them in utter and complete shock. "So… we're all okay with this, right? I mean, we all know I'm sleeping with all of you, right?"

"Well, not all at once. Gross," Rafe replies, wrinkling his nose. "That's a little bit too much of a sausage-fest for me. But yeah, it's all good."

"I would never tie you down. This arrangement is fine with me. Though the point about sausage is a valid one," Tomás agrees.

Scott laughs. "I feel you there. As long as my time with you is our own, I don't have a problem."

"You know already that I was hoping you'd see other men, little red bird," Damien says. "My schedule just isn't conducive to a different sort of relationship. And, as Rafe says, these are all good men. And STD-free."

Tomás, Rafe, and Scott all stare at Damien. "Did you have our medical records pulled?" Scott asks, bewildered.

Damien shrugs. "I like to be in the know."

"If you weren't on our side, you would be a very scary man," Rafe murmurs, and Tomás nods along to his statement.

"Then it's a good thing we're all on the same side," Damien chuckles darkly. He starts laughing for real after silence falls. "The looks on your faces! Oh, that's going to carry me all through the week."

"Ha ha," Rafe mutters.

I kiss my other three men goodbye and then take Damien's arm.

TWENTY

Pent Up in the Penthouse

Harper

I lie in the back of Damien's town car with my head in his lap, keeping myself below the windows just in case Jack is lurking somewhere, watching. If he still thinks I'm at Scott's farm, all the better. Damien left a bodyguard there to help with the situation, just in case my ex shows up again and things get ugly. The remaining two bodyguards are with us, sitting up front, serious as stone.

Damien strokes my hair, letting the tendrils run through his fingers. "Everything's going to be okay, little red bird," he says quietly. "I'm going to take care of it. He won't bother you anymore."

I look up at him, and his eyes narrow. He runs a thumb over the bruise on my arm. It's an ugly shade of purple and green.

"Did he do this?" he asks.

With a swallow, I nod my head.

"Hmm. It makes me far less amenable to letting him live," he grumbles.

"Like Tomás said, he's not worth the stain on your soul," I reply, squeezing his knee. I don't think he'd actually put a hit on someone. He's rich, not a member of the mafia, but now I'm wondering.

"Hmm," he murmurs again. Then he sighs. "You're probably right. Killing a policeman probably comes with… baggage."

I take Damien's other hand and squeeze it, my eyelids getting droopy with his soft attention to my hair. "Have… have you had to have people killed before?"

He smiles. "Of course not, but I'd do anything for you."

I want to know more, but I don't want to push him, so I just nod, my cheek rubbing against his thigh.

"Someday, maybe we'll revisit this conversation," he tells me. "But you don't need to worry about it." He tugs my hair and meets my eyes with his green ones.

"Do you think it's safe to sit up?" I whisper, glancing at the bodyguards before running my tongue over the front of his pants.

Damien hisses. "Close the partition," he orders the bodyguards sharply.

The partition goes up, and Damien pulls his zipper down. His cock springing out to greet me.

I start to take it in my mouth, desperately wanting a distraction from my situation, but he tugs on my hair again.

"You're not wearing underwear," he says with complete certainty.

"I… uh… lost them in Scott's barn." I sigh. "I swear it's not my fault."

"Remind me to thank him." He runs a finger down my cheek. "You know, you don't have to do this, if you don't want to. I'm happy to help you, regardless."

I stroke his cock from base to tip and down again. "I know. I want to. I want you to make me feel good. I want to forget for a little while."

"Then you're going to be doing a lot of forgetting tonight." Damien shifts so I'm underneath him.

My knees go up on either side of his waist, wide to make room for him. My skirt has slid down a little, but Damien works it the rest of the way to my waist. He's kneeling up a bit, also trying to make room for himself in the back of the sedan, and puts an arm under my hips to raise me up enough to take his cock. I wrap my arms around his neck and move my hips to meet his thrusts.

"Oh, yes, my little red bird. Just like that. Show me what I've been missing," he groans. He sucks my neck, nibbling my skin while slamming his cock into me in a desperate frenzy.

"I-I've missed you too," I gasp, my nails digging into his skin. It's all I can do to keep up while he rides me.

"Take all of it," he commands me. "Tell me how much you want me to make you come."

I moan. "Please." I'm right on the edge. "Please, make me come."

Damien bites my nipple through the dress and I come, crying out, "Fuck!"

"God, you feel so good." He sighs, thrusting deep inside me to keep me floating on my high while his cum spills into me.

When both of us have ridden out every tiny tremor, he finally stops, his semi-hard dick still buried deep inside me.

"God, how much did you miss me?" I ask, panting as I cling to him.

He doesn't answer right away. Instead, he slides his hand up under the bodice of my dress and thumbs my stinging nipple.

I make a sound of pleasure and pain in my throat.

"I missed you a great deal, little red bird," he says.

* * *

DAMIEN

I probably shouldn't still have an erection after having it so good with Harper. But I guess my body didn't get that memo because I'm as stiff as a flagpole within fifteen minutes of ejaculating inside her. There is just something about Harper. I can't get enough.

I know she can feel me hardening inside her. And God bless this woman, she simply tugs down the cap sleeves of her dress, and the wide neckline descends beneath her beautiful breasts. Venus de Milo has nothing on Harper's breasts. I want to consume them. To consume her.

"Damien, are you going to fuck me again?" she asks, batting her eyelashes at me.

I'm straining inside her, probably leaking, and she's teasing me about that? *Naughty girl.* "Yes, little red bird. I'm going to fuck you all—"

The partition comes down just enough for Marco's voice to carry. "Sir, we've arrived."

Harper covers her breasts, even though Marco can't see anything through the tiny crack. I sigh and slip my hand under one of her hands to fondle her breast. Regretfully, I say, "I guess we're here."

"I guess," she answers in a strained tone.

With a grunt, I pull out of her. My dick is quite unhappy to be going back in my pants, and I have to be careful about zipping up, but I do get myself back together.

She watches my every move.

I give her my best sexy smile. "We'll continue this upstairs."

I pull up her bodice and twitch down her skirt. There's a wet spot on her dress from all our activities, so I put my suit jacket around her when we get out of the car to cover the evidence.

"We'll be in the lobby, sir," Marco says as the two of them escort us to the elevator. "Please call if you need us."

"Of course," I reply. I put a hand at Harper's back to guide her into the elevator. When the doors close, my hand slides down to cup her ass.

She laughs and looks up at me with those beautiful aquamarine eyes of hers. "Let me guess. One of your fantasies is to do it in an elevator."

I've actually done it in an elevator before, but I decide that's not a bad idea now. I push the STOP button.

The elevator jerks to a stop.

Harper stares at me, eyes and mouth wide with shock. "You're serious."

"As a heart attack," I quip, taking my jacket off her and draping it over a rail.

"You seriously want to do it in an elevator?" She gasps.

I begin unbuttoning my pants. "Yes."

"But… we… what if someone needs it?" she objects.

I open my fly and my beleaguered cock springs out of its prison. "We need it."

"But—"

"Little red bird, take off your dress," I order.

She swallows, then complies. "Yes, Damien." The dress hits the floor, leaving her in strappy heeled white sandals and nothing else.

"I really am going to need to send Scott a thank you card," I murmur, backing her to the wall. Her body is mine for the taking, and I intend to take full advantage. Of course, there's a camera in here, but no one would dare watch me fuck this beauty.

The elevator has mirrored walls on three sides, excluding the door. "Grab the bar," I tell her.

Harper shivers and grips the hand rail at the back of the elevator. "Yes, sir."

"Bend forward and spread your legs," I instruct, smoothing a hand down her bare ass.

She does as she's told with another, "Yes, Damien."

"Now, hang on tight." I plunge my dick into that sweet little pussy of hers.

"Oh, God," she gasps, gripping the railing as I start ramming her. I'm merciless–and she loves it.

I grip her chin and bring her head up. "Watch," I say, kissing her cheek as I force her to look into the mirror.

Her breasts sway with every hard thrust. In the side mirrors, we can both see my cock ramming in and out.

She reaches back and grabs my thigh with one hand, keeping herself braced with the other. "Don't stop, Damien. Fill me up. PLEASE."

I delve my hand down between her legs and rub her clit so she can see in the mirror as I ravage her hole. "I've got you, little red bird. I will always give you what you need."

Harper whimpers, reaching behind her, and her nails dig into my thigh with a delicious sting .I rub her clit harder, and she cries out.

"No, no looking down." I tilt her chin up again. "I want you to see how beautiful you are when you come."

I can tell it takes her some effort, but Harper does as I tell her. In two thrusts and another tweak of her clit, she's coming apart around me, milking my dick for my cum, and I give it to her, though I keep thrusting until she's completely spent.

I slide my dick out of her, now finally sated, and I lean my chin on her shoulder, kissing her temple as I fondle her breasts, watching in the mirror. "Do you see how beautiful you are?"

She nods slowly, still panting. "Yes, Damien."

The comm on the elevator goes off. "Is everything all right in there?"

"Just fine. No need to worry," I call back while Harper hurriedly snatches up her dress. "We'll be on our way again in just a second."

I pull up my pants and get the elevator going again. "You are *so* bad," she whispers to me.

"So are you," I murmur back. I squeeze her ass as a little old lady and her Pekingese board the elevator on the next floor.

Harper frowns at me but doesn't swat my hand away.

"Good girl." I grin.

TWENTY-ONE

Homecoming for One

Harper

I've changed into jeans and a T-shirt for the ride back to my apartment. Damien bought some clothes just for me after our first date. Honestly, I'm afraid to wear anything with easy access. Damien kept me up all night, and then had me again this morning, into the afternoon. He has an insatiable appetite for every area of his life. He's still giving me the most wolfish grin as we ride in the town car. I frown at him. "I hope you're proud of yourself. I didn't get a wink of sleep!"

"I'm quite proud, actually. Thank you for asking." He chuckles.

I swat his shoulder, and he captures my hand and nibbles my fingertips. Now, I'm wishing I *had* worn something more accessible.

"Too bad you're not wearing a skirt today. Though I must say, your ass looks great in those jeans," he says when he releases my hand.

"Thanks." I shake my head at him. "I can't believe we did it so many times last night. And today. How do you keep going like that?"

He shrugs. "You inspire me."

Aww, that's sweet. My heart gets a little melty.

"Don't you give me that gooey look. I'll try to smuggle you in my carry-on luggage back to New York," he warns me.

I snort. "You fly in a jet."

Damien lets out a bark of laughter. "Good point. I do."

I lean my head on his shoulder, and my eyelids droop.

He kisses my hair. "You're not going to have enough time for that. You can take a nap when we get to your apartment. Assuming Tomás isn't feeling overly frisky."

"You four are going to be the death of me! You know that, right?" I groan.

"*La petite mort*," he teases me.

"I didn't take French," I remind him.

Damien nibbles my ear. "You still know what it means."

"Yeah, I do." The little death. The French had it right all along. I'm pretty sure one day I'm going to die of a fantastic orgasm with one of these guys.

"So worldly." He smirks at me.

"I guess my special gift is knowing international euphemisms for 'orgasm,'" I quip.

He chuckles. "A worthy talent."

The car stops in the back of the apartment building where the most-used entrance is. I look in the parking lot and blink when I see the car I share with McKenzy. "You've all been busy."

"Tomás and Scott took care of that. We all thought it best they take your car back here while I took you to my penthouse. Bait and switch and all that. But no one reported seeing Jack or his vehicle, which is good," he says.

Damien gets out of the town car and comes around the side, waiting for Marco to open my door. Then he takes my hand and pulls me out of the car and against his body.

"Now you're just trying to be naughty," I scold him. "And out in broad daylight too!"

"You love it when I'm naughty," he reminds me and kisses me, then gives my ass a squeeze before letting me go. "Come on, let's go upstairs."

I'm half afraid and half hopeful that we're going to fuck again until Tomás gets here. I realize I'm developing an appetite more voracious than Damien's!

However, when we get to the apartment, Scott, Tomás, and Rafe are already there, waiting outside.

"Sorry for being a little tardy," Damien says to the other men as he scoots me along with a hand at my back.

"That's okay. There's an art crawl of some sort happening in St. Paul today, so the building was unlocked. That doesn't give me a lot of faith in security around here," Tomás grumbles. "McKenzy isn't back yet. Or, if she is, she's decided not to let us in."

That doesn't sound right. I take out my key and unlock the door. "McKenzy?" I call.

No one answers. The apartment is empty.

"We told her we'd be here at one," Scott says. "But she's with her parents. Maybe she decided to stay there a little while longer?"

"McKenzy is always fashionably late." I sigh. "So are her parents. It doesn't surprise me that they haven't dropped her off yet."

The men nod. "All right. Let's check this place for that asshole. Then we can order pizza," Rafe suggests.

"I haven't had pizza in a very long time. It sounds delicious," Damien responds. They all fan out and start to search through the apartment.

With nothing else to do but worry Jack is going to come popping out of a closet, I sit down in the living room on one of McKenzy's more flashy creations. I feel bad for making her miss the art crawl. She loves to show off her furniture.

"Is that even… comfortable?" Scott asks, wrinkling his nose at the twisted chair I'm sitting on. He looks around at the rest of the seating. "Is *any* of this comfortable?"

"You'd be surprised." I get up and gesture for him to sit.

Scott sits down and blinks. "Wow, I'm impressed."

"Her furniture might look a bit different, but she always designs around comfort," I inform him, proud of my friend and her art.

Tomás and Damien reappear, but Rafe is still off in another room. His swearing signals me that he's in McKenzy's room.

"Sorry!" I call. "She's kind of a clothes horse."

Rafe stomps out with his hair sticking out at odd angles. "She's an everything horse. I could barely get to her bed to check underneath it!"

I wince. "Yeah, but she assures me there's a method to her madness."

"I'm just seeing madness, but it's her bedroom." Rafe is just coming to sit down when Tomás draws a sharp breath.

"*Que maravilloso*," he breathes from the windows.

I spin around. Tomás has silently made his way over to the corner where I work. He's holding the sheet I'd draped over the canvas I was working on and staring at the unfinished painting.

"Hey now!" I protest.

Damien and Rafe make their way over. Scott rises to do the same, and all four men stand there, admiring my work.

"Wow, sugar. I knew you were good but this is… really something," Rafe compliments me.

"Indeed. Seeing your work in person rather than on your phone is quite the experience," Damien agrees.

Scott seems to have been struck speechless.

Tomás has found the corner where I keep my finished works and is rifling through them.

"Do you mind?!" I ask, going over.

"Where do you display these?" Tomás enquires. "*Mi preciosa*, you say you are becoming more popular on the art scene…"

I feel a tickle of air on the back of my neck. Rafe and Damien have come over to see my other works as well.

Scott is still transfixed by the unfinished one.

"I sell them at the Witch's Brew," I grumble. "You really don't have to go through all of these."

"We most certainly do." Damien gently hands one to Rafe to look at.

"Is this one for anyone in particular? I want to buy it when it's done," Scott finally murmurs.

I give up on hiding my artwork from my men and go over to

Scott. "It's not for anyone in particular," I say, putting a hand on his shoulder. "Well, it is now. It's for you."

"How much do these usually cost?" Scott asks.

"I'd never charge you. Any of you. You mean too much to me," I reply.

The others catch what I say and come scurrying over with paintings. Well, Rafe and Tomás scurry. I don't think Damien could ever do something so undignified. But he's holding a painting just like the other two.

"I will buy them all," Damien says. "And each of you can have one. Something so special must be shared."

I blush. I'm pretty sure he's talking about more than the paintings. "Really, I couldn't accept money from any of you. Okay, maybe if you want more than one. But it… I feel good knowing you have something of mine, you know?"

Tomás hugs me. "*Gracias,* Helena."

"Why do you sometimes call her Helena?" Scott asks. "That's not her name."

"It was her name in Spanish class," Rafe clarifies before Tomás can answer.

I raise an eyebrow at Rafe. "I can't believe you remember that!"

"I remember the important things." He smiles softly.

Damien rolls his eyes. "This is all very cute and all, but I believe I was promised pizza?"

"Right." Rafe takes out his phone and opens an app. "What's everybody's order?"

We all crowd around Rafe and choose pizza toppings as well as breadsticks and dessert. Rafe orders a few sodas as well.

By the time the pizza comes, and we're finished eating, it's almost four.

"This is a bit more fashionably late than McKenzy usually is," I note worriedly, glancing at my phone. The sound is on, but I'm still hoping against hope I've missed a message from her.

Damien's phone rings, and I look up, hope blossoming in my chest.

"Hmm." Damien talks to whoever is on the other end of the line in a clipped tone. "Yes. Hmm. Good. That's good."

"Is it McKenzy?" I ask while he's still grunting at the other person. I don't know why she'd call him and not me, but I'm hopeful.

Damien shakes his head. My stomach plummets, and I suddenly feel sick. He hangs up and sets his phone down. "Jack has been suspended without pay from the Otsego Police Department."

"That's good," Rafe says.

"He's disappeared," Damien adds.

"That's not so good," Rafe replies.

I get a bad feeling in my gut. "Where is McKenzy?"

"Her bodyguards reported in about two o'clock. She was just getting in the car with her father," Damien tells me. He taps his fingers on the countertop. "I must say, I'm a bit worried myself."

"So, ask her bodyguards where she is," Rafe presses.

"I did. They haven't responded to my text." Damien stops tapping his fingers. "I'm going to call a PI I know and see if he can find Jack. As for McKenzy, I don't want you to worry yet. A number of things could have happened. I'll find out and get back to you."

Tomás rubs my back. "You look very tired. Is it from all the stress?"

"Sure…" I respond, my eyes shooting daggers at Damien. "Stress."

"Is that what the kids are calling it these days?" Scott grins.

Rafe bursts out laughing, but even his laughter has an edge to it. We're all worried about McKenzy.

Tomás moves his hand up to the back of my neck and gives me the most wonderful neck massage. "We can't do anything right now, *mi preciosa.* You need rest. Come on, let's get you into bed."

"I've got two bodyguards downstairs," Rafe says. "I'll have them come up and guard the door. You're safe, sugar."

"But… what about McKenzy?" I ask.

"I'll find her," Damien promises. "Just leave it to me."

I'm not sure I want to just leave it to him. I want to be out with a Bloodhound searching for her. I know logically, however, that

Damien will have a better chance of finding her than I will. Even with a Bloodhound. "Okay," I relent.

"Excellent. Go with Tomás, and get some rest. Rafe, I swear if you screw up my points for Fantasy Football by missing practice this week, I will buy your team just so I can become your own personal nightmare," Damien warns him.

Rafe winks at him. "Wouldn't dream of it."

"Good," Scott agrees. "You're one of my top picks. I've got fifty bucks riding on your next game."

"I have…significantly more," Damien says.

"Oh, rub it in, why don't you?" Scott chuckles.

Damien smirks and stands. "I have work to do. I think you two do as well. Let's get out of Harper's hair so she can get some sleep."

"Good plan," Scott agrees. He heads for the door with Damien, who is carrying a painting.

"You stay safe, sugar. Don't go doing anything crazy," Rafe says before picking up his painting as well. It's scary sometimes how well Rafe knows me.

"I'll try," I mumble noncommittally.

"Let Damien find McKenzy. Everything's going to be okay," Rafe promises then also leaves.

Then it's just Tomás and me.

TWENTY-TWO

Cold Comfort

Harper

"You should really get some sleep, *mi preciosa*," Tomás advises kindly, sitting down next to me on the sofa. "I think maybe Damien kept you up for a long time, no?"

I lean against his shoulder. I mean, he's not wrong, but.... "What about McKenzy?"

"I will wake you up if I hear anything," he says, taking my hands in his. "Maybe her parents wanted to take her somewhere else, and she forgot to check in. Now, *cariña*, you must get some rest."

He stands and pulls me up with him. Then he wraps an arm around my shoulders and guides me to my bedroom.

I look at the carefully made bed and think of McKenzy's messy one. It just feels so uncomfortable not having her here. "Maybe I should stay up a while."

"No. I promise I will wake you if I get any information," Tomás insists firmly as he pulls my covers back.

The bed does look very inviting. "Promise?"

"I promise." Tomás crosses his heart.

"Okay." I start stripping, yanking my shirt over my head and wriggling out of my jeans. Today, for once, I did wear a bra. I didn't think it would help the situation if Damien was looking at my bouncing breasts while we drove to the apartment.

I am also wearing the closest thing I have to granny panties—lacy full briefs—but that doesn't seem to bother Tomás one bit. He swallows hard as he watches me take off my clothes.

"You said you wanted me to go to bed," I remind him as I unsnap my bra.

His eyes go wide and hungry when I reveal my breasts. He licks his lips, then squeezes his eyes shut. "Get in bed now, Helena, or there will be consequences."

"What sort of consequences?" I ask with feigned innocence.

"Good God," he groans and pulls me against his body. "You drive a man completely *loco*!"

I hadn't been thinking about sex, but Tomás pressed against me does raise new possibilities in my mind. I'm suddenly not tired. "Really? Do tell."

"Helena, you are supposed to be sleeping," he says, trying to sound stern, but there is a hint of desperation in his tone.

"Hmm." I flick open the button on his fly.

Tomás groans and grabs my wrist. "Aren't you tired, *mi preciosa*?"

"Not anymore." I lock eyes with him while I tug his zipper down.

He lets me, though he keeps his hand on my wrist, so it's sort of like we're doing it together.

"Glad you agree with me." I smile. I reach into his boxers and scoop out his dick.

He's so excited he leaks a little on my palm. "Helena…"

I use the precum as lube to stroke his cock, swirling my thumb around the tip to get more with every upstroke.

"Dios mío," Tomás gasps, his hand still on my wrist as I jerk him off. "Please, no more. I'm about to burst!"

"Where do you want to burst?" I ask.

Tomás cups my pussy through the lacy briefs I'm wearing. "Here. I want to cum inside you, *mi cariña*."

"I think that can be arranged." I let go of his dick so I can slide my panties down to my ankles and kick them off.

In the amount of time it takes me to do that, he gets completely undressed, socks, boxers, pants, shirt, everything flying to different corners of my room.

"You're in a hurry." I grin.

"*Sí, mi preciosa*. I am," he tells me in a strained tone. He grabs me by the shoulders and pushes me down on the bed.

"You can just go right in," I murmur to him as his fingers creep down over my belly toward the promised land. "I'm ready."

Tomás is still courteous and curls two fingers inside me. He groans. "You're sure?" he asks, stroking the spot where I want to be touched the most.

"Positive," I moan, thinking of his dick rubbing inside me.

He withdraws his fingers, then lifts one of my legs over his hip and slowly pushes into me. He stretches me wide with every inch he gives me.

I grip the sheets, crying out as my body struggles, then succeeds in taking him in. He doesn't hit so deep, but my God, the girth of this man!

"So nice and tight," Tomás hisses, grasping my hips so our bodies are completely fused.

"Please," I beg him after he holds us still in that position a few moments longer than I have the patience for. "I want you so bad."

He kisses me, then gives me exactly what I need. He pounds me, just like he did on the desk in his office.

I twist my fingers in the sheets and wrap my legs around his waist, holding on for dear life. The pressure builds and builds, and finally, the fireworks start.

"Oh, my God!" I scream as my inner muscles clamp around his cock. My whole body shakes, both with the force of his thrusts and the strength of my orgasm.

But he doesn't finish. Instead, he fucks me harder.

* * *

TOMÁS

It's not enough. I need more. I need more of her tight pussy. I don't want to stop. I don't ever want to stop.

Of course, that's not a possibility, and after she moans one more time, her muscles fisting around *mi* cock like a vice, I give it up. I explode inside her with a groan.

Panting, sweaty, spent, we curl up on the bed together and snuggle into each other's arms. I decide snuggling is nice. There really wasn't much of that after I banged her on my desk.

I don't think my wife and I snuggled for years. Toward the end, she treated sex like an onerous duty. Helena is an enthusiastic partner. Beautiful, adventurous, but also kind-hearted and loyal. I wish I hadn't been married when we first met. If I'd allowed myself to know her then the way I know her now, I would have fucked the stuffing out of her everywhere. Outdoors. Indoors. On furniture. Against trees… so many wasted years with that cheating bitch, Carmen! But then, I wouldn't have been allowed to date a student, so maybe it's best it's all a fantasy.

"What are you thinking about?" she asks me.

Caught. "Um… well… outdoor sex, actually." I cough, not wanting to lie to her. "With you."

She thumbs my nipple gently, kissing my neck. "Where would you like to do it, *Profe*?"

Up for anything. I love it. I return the favor, sliding my hand down over her ass and squeezing playfully. "Just about anywhere, actually. As long as it's with you."

"You're a very sweet man, *Profe*." She smiles, and it's like a sunrise over my decimated life. I thought for sure I would never love again, but it would be easy to love her.

Before I say something foolish, I kiss her.

She kisses me back and my cock decides it wants another go. Not just my cock. I like being close with her.

My heart is in real danger.

"You went somewhere," she whispers, brushing a stray bit of hair from my forehead. "What's wrong?"

I swallow, afraid to discuss such feelings so soon. To say I am gun-shy is a vast understatement.

Thankfully, I am saved from the conversation by Camisa Negra playing from my phone. "I'm getting a call," I say and wriggle my arm out from under her so I can get up and go hunt for my pants.

"I hope it's about McKenzy," she says, sitting up, holding the blanket to her chest with one hand. As if I haven't seen, touched, and tasted everything.

"I hope so, too." I finally yank my phone out of my pants pocket. It's Damien. *"Hello?"*

"McKenzy is missing," he rushes in without mincing words. "Her parents' car was found not three blocks away from the house. Both of them are fine, but were knocked unconscious. McKenzy is gone."

"Mierda." I look over at Helena. "I'll let Harper know."

"Don't let her leave the apartment. I know she's going to try to do something crazy like go out looking for her, but I've got that all under control." His tone is tight, and it doesn't sound as though anything is in his control right now.

"Bueno," I agree just the same. "I won't let her out of my sight."

"I've also given instructions to the bodyguards outside not to let her leave," he adds. "Just in case she gets the better of you. She's a wily one, our Harper."

"Sí, she is," I say.

Damien then hangs up, but he never struck me as a man who dawdled on the phone.

"What's happened? Why do you need to keep an eye on me?" she demands.

I sit down on the bed and take her hands. "McKenzy is missing."

"What?" She tries to pull her hands back, but I hold firm. "Missing? When? How long?"

"Since her bodyguards last checked in" I reply. "Damien is taking care of it. We just need to stay here and remain calm."

"Calm? *Calm?* How the hell am I supposed to do that?" she asks.

I squeeze her hands. "You need to breathe, Helena. Breathe." She doesn't want to, but we do end up taking several deep breaths together. "*Bueno.* We're going to stay here and wait to hear from Damien again. He is taking care of everything," I tell her, keeping my voice level.

"Is he? Then where's McKenzy?" she grumbles.

"He's working on it. Have a little faith," I respond.

She doesn't look convinced.

"He's a very powerful man. If anyone can find her, he can," I reassure her.

"I suppose that's true." She frowns. "But we all have a pretty good idea of what happened to her, I think."

"Damien will find Jack." I know this much is true. And I wouldn't want to be Jack when this happens.

"Will he find him in time?" she asks shrewdly.

I have to stop myself from shrugging. That will just make the whole situation blow up. "He will try, *mi preciosa.*"

"Jack wants me. All we have to do is find a way to trade," she continues.

My blood freezes at the very idea. "That's not happening."

"Oh? What, you think you can stop me?" She puffs up her chest.

Her breasts are lovely, but she's lovelier, and I'm not about to lose her on my watch. "Helena, *mi cariña,* I will duct tape you to this bed if I have to. You are not leaving this apartment."

"You wouldn't dare!" She scoffs at me.

TWENTY-THREE

All Tied Up

Harper

I don't think he's serious. I really don't. Until I see his eyes darken.

"Oh shit." I scramble over to the other side of the bed, putting it between me and Tomás.

"*Cariña*, I'm not going to duct tape you to the bed," he sighs.

"Uh-huh. I don't believe you," I respond, still keeping the bed between us.

Tomás rolls his eyes. "I would have used something far less abrasive."

"What?" I yell.

"I'm kidding. But if me standing here will keep you from trying to leave the apartment, all the better," he says.

I narrow my eyes at him. "You're on, *Profe*."

With a slight smile, he stands in front of the door with his arms crossed. "And just what do you think you can do?"

He's not Rafe, so he's not built like a football player, but that doesn't mean he's some skinny little thing either. He has muscles. I know because I've seen and felt them all.

I'm not completely helpless by any stretch of the imagination, but it occurs to me that my men are still stronger than I am. I'll have to outwit him before…

I hear the front door open and the shuffle of feet. Rafe is talking about something with Scott.

"You were just trying to distract me!" I object.

Tomás shrugs. "I didn't know they were coming, but this is most fortuitous, yes."

The bedroom door opens and bumps Tomás in the back. Rafe sticks his head in and says. "I thought you might be in here. You look gorgeous as always, sugar. All naked and… ewww, Tomás, put some pants on!"

Tomás blushes and hurries to put on his boxers.

I fold my arms over my chest so Rafe has to stop ogling my breasts. "Did Damien call you?"

"He thought Tomás could use some backup, yeah." Rafe pouts. "But your nipples were all pink and swollen and everything."

"Rafe, you guys can't just keep me here! Jack's got McKenzy!" I yell.

"We don't know that for certain," Tomás replies, making a 'calm down' motion with his hands.

I put my hands on my hips, which means two sets of eyes are now staring at my chest. "We don't know that for certain? Who do we think has her then, the Easter Bunny?"

"What's all the yelling about?" Scott pops his head around the door as well. "I like the view, but what's the problem?"

"Harper's trying to tell us why we should let her go out looking for McKenzy. Right?" Rafe asks.

That man knows me far too well, but then, I wasn't going to fool Tomás, and Scott is just nodding his head as though he's not surprised.

"You can't do that," Scott adds his voice to the naysayers. "It's too dangerous."

"McKenzy's in trouble. You can't just expect me to sit here!"

Three identical stern expressions tell me that yes, they do just expect me to sit here.

"Come on!" I argue. "You can't—"

"We can. We are. We will." I'd been so busy shouting at the other three, I hadn't even heard Damien's arrival. He taps the door all the way open with the toe of his very expensive leather shoe, revealing that now all four of them are here to stop me.

I glance from face to face, searching for some sign of solidarity with my cause. But all of them are on the same page "But…"

"Have you eaten recently?" Damien asks.

I hunch my shoulders. "No." I'm not pouting. I'm not.

"I'll make you something," Scott says. "You come on out when you're ready."

Tomás pulls on his pants and shirt, and follows Scott and Damien out into the living room.

Rafe stays.

"It's for the best, sugar," he tells me.

I throw a pillow at him.

The stupid football player deftly catches it. "Go on. Get dressed. Scott's making you something to eat."

Swearing under my breath, I give Rafe a defiant look and stomp into the shower instead.

The bastard has the audacity to chuckle!

Whatever. I scrub myself off and then get dressed. Rafe has disappeared, but I can hear him out in the kitchen talking with the other men.

I flounce out of my bedroom in jeans and a baggy T-shirt that fully covers my ass. No eye candy for them! My hair is pulled back in a severe bun, so they'll know I mean business.

They all look up. Damien raises an eyebrow, his lips twitching. Scott coughs to try to hide a laugh. Tomás covers his mouth, but his eyes are twinkling. Rafe doesn't bother with politeness. He openly guffaws.

"What?" I snap at him.

"You're just so cute." Rafe grins. "Like that getup is going to stop any one of us from wanting to jump your bones."

I feel my cheeks flush with anger, but pointedly ignore him. I take the stool at the island counter between Tomás and Rafe. "What are we eating?" I ask Scott.

He sets a plate with the most delicious-looking omelet and three strips of bacon in front of me. My mouth waters.

"Eat up," Scott encourages. "Pretty sure you're going to need your strength."

I am, but not because I am letting Rafe have his way with me during his rotation. Oh no. The Harper Store is closed.

"Thanks." I start wolfing down the omelet. It's just as good as it looks.

Tomás puts a hand on my knee. "Helena," he murmurs. "Please don't be mad."

"Of course I'm mad! You all won't let me go find McKenzy." I huff around a mouthful of eggs.

"And just where did you intend to start?" Damien asks. "I still haven't confirmed whether or not she's even with Jack, much less managed to locate him. He's disappeared."

I open my mouth to give a smart retort, but nothing comes out. Where exactly do I intend to start? My shoulders slump in defeat.

Rafe massages them, trying to comfort me. "Damien's men are going to find them both, sugar. We just need to be patient. He's got everybody you could possibly think of out looking for them."

"Twenty-three private investigators and half the police force," Scott confirms.

I suddenly feel a bit like a petulant child. I look up at Damien. "Thank you," I say, cursing myself for my tremulous tone.

"Little red bird, I would do this for you any time in a heartbeat," Damien replies, reaching over to squeeze my hand.

I finally can't take it anymore. I burst into tears.

Damien and Scott come around the island and join Tomás and Rafe in giving me a group hug. I cling to them for a while then wriggle myself free.

"I need some time," I choke out. "I'm going up to the patio."

"All right, *cariña*. We understand," Tomás says kindly.

"Marco will go with you," Damien adds.

I snort. "What, so I can't escape?"

"Yes," Damien responds without a hint of regret.

"You just kind of pretend bodyguards are invisible, sugar," Rafe advises me.

"We'll be here when you get back." Scott gives my hand another squeeze.

I sigh, knowing they're all doing their best. I should be grateful they're all here. But I'm getting a bit annoyed at their overprotectiveness. "Okay," I grumble and march away from the kitchen and out the door.

Marco does, indeed, peel off from the wall beside the door and follow me up to the shared patio on the roof. He stands unobtrusively next to the door, and I stand in the middle of the space with my arms folded, trying to gather my thoughts. To gather myself.

McKenzy is missing, and it's all my fault.

Tears roll down my cheeks again, unbidden. I rub them away. They're not going to help the situation. I try to remind myself that I don't know for sure that she's been taken, but I'm so worried about her.

My phone suddenly rings, making me jump. I forgot I put it in my pocket!

I fish it out and look at the screen. *Unknown Number.*

I'm pretty sure I know who it is. With a sense of dread, I answer it. "Hello?"

"Harper?! Harper, don't do anything he sa—" McKenzy's sobbing voice greets me before being abruptly cut off.

"Are you alone?" Jack demands to know.

"No," I reply, my heart pounding so loud in my ears I can barely hear him. I don't know if I'm more angry or terrified.

"I'm sure I don't have to tell you how serious I am," Jack continues. "Don't let on that it's me."

"Of course not, Mom," I say.

"Good girl."

I scowl. Only Damien gets to call me 'good girl.'

"What can I do for you?"

"You can meet me at the abandoned creamery in Hastings," he responds. "Come alone—or else."

McKenzy lets out a scream in the background, and my blood

boils. "You don't have to do that." I keep my voice pleasant though I want to murder him.

"I know. I just wanted to make sure you understood the situation," Jack says. "Leave your phone. Or toss it, I don't care. I don't want that asshole Blackwood tracking your location."

"I understand." I step toward the edge of the patio and lean against the railing.

"Good. See you soon." McKenzy screams again just before Jack hangs up.

I wish I owned a gun and that I knew how to use it. I take the phone from my ear and, ever-so-innocently, let it slip from my fingers, clattering and shattering stories beneath me. "Oh no!" I cry.

Marco comes over. "What is it?"

"I'm such an idiot. I dropped my phone!" I lament.

"Damien will get you a new one." He shrugs. "Looks like that one's toast."

"Are you sure?" I ask anxiously. "I want to be able to take the call if McKenzy reaches out."

Marco leans over a bit further, frowning at the phone fragments below. "I really don't think—"

I kick him as hard as I can in the back of the knee, and his leg buckles. He lets out a surprised grunt and reaches for me, but I'm too fast.

"Sorry!" I shout over my shoulder as I sprint for the patio door. I close and lock it behind me just as he throws his full weight against it. The metal door shakes ominously, but holds.

I know I have less than no time. I pelt down the stairs, just in case it's within Damien's power to stop the elevator, and run out the back entrance to the parking lot. Our car is there, just where Tomás and Scott left it.

I don't have my keys on me—I'm sure Damien would have taken them if I did—but I know a secret they don't. I wrench open the fuel door, and the spare key falls into my outstretched palm.

Maybe Damien can track my car. Maybe a cop will pull me over. But I'm going to give this my best effort. It's not like Jack can fault me for trying, right?

I unlock the car, hop in behind the wheel, and tear out of the parking lot just as I see the other bodyguard and my four men burst out the back door.

I snap my seat belt into place while driving. By some miracle, I make it to the highway without getting caught. It takes everything in me, but I drive the speed limit. I can't get caught. Not now.

I'm more grateful than ever that McKenzy and I have a popular vehicle. I pass at least two others as I head south.

Thirty-five white-knuckled minutes later, I'm on Vermillion Street in Hastings. I pass their quaint little downtown neighborhood, a couple of churches, and a rehab center before I find the creamery next to an old tourist attraction mansion called The LeDuc. I park on the side street next to the mansion so the car remains inconspicuous for as long as possible.

I lean my forehead on the steering wheel and take several deep breaths.

Then I get out to face my destiny.

TWENTY-FOUR

Flying the Coop

Damien

"Well, this is inconvenient," I say as the four of us stand out in the parking lot like fools, looking at the spot the car should be parked as though staring at it will make it reappear.

"Inconvenient? Man, you need to up your vocabulary. This is a disaster!" Rafe sighs, shaking his head. "What the fuck happened anyway?"

"Marco says she got a call from her mother," I reply. "Of course that was a lie. She got a call from a burner phone. Doubtless it was Jack. She kicked him and ran away. "

Tomás groans. "I must agree with Rafe. This is a disaster."

"How are we going to find her? Where do you think he sent her? Is the burner phone still on?" Scott asks.

I pull up Harper's location on my phone. "It would appear," I say, holding my phone up for them to see. "She is heading south."

"Oh, so she didn't turn off her phone. Smart," Rafe decides.

"Marco says she dropped it over the rail of the patio." I shrug.

Scott frowns. "Then how do you know her location?"

"I have a tracker on her car," I explain.

Their looks range from shocked to judgmental.

"Does she know you're stalking her?" Rafe asks.

"Yes. But she doesn't know about the device. Good thing too." I upload Harper's locator info to the investigators and police I've commandeered to find her. "Now, whose car are we riding in?"

"You're scary," Rafe comments. "I'm glad you're on our side."

Tomás jangles his keys. "Let's go!"

Given he drives a Volvo, I wonder if there will be enough room for all of us, but we'll manage. "Get Marco and follow us to her location," I order Pete. "I will be riding in the Volvo."

Pete nearly chokes on his tongue. "A… Volvo, sir?"

"Yes. Now go." I quickly stride after the other three who are already clambering into Tomás's car.

Rafe allows me to ride shotgun. He and Scott get in the back.

"Buckle up," Tomás says before pressing his foot down on the gas.

I grip the seat belt and finally manage to put it on between Tomás's careening out of the parking lot and then quickly onto the highway going south. The man obviously missed his calling as a NASCAR driver.

"Damn. Remind me never to let you drive my car," Rafe wheezes.

"Don't listen to him. You're doing a wonderful job, Tomás," I add, though my nails are digging into my thighs. He's at least going to get us there in time.

I hope.

* * *

HARPER

I go to the front door of the creamery, but it's locked. Circling around the side and back, I try the doors until one opens. I step inside the darkened building and try to see something. Anything.

"McKenzy?" I call. "Jack?"

Out of the shadows, Jack steps into the light of the open door. He's got McKenzy in front of him and is holding a gun to her head. "Harper. Did you come alone?"

"Yes," I reply. "Now, you've got me. Let McKenzy go."

"Get out of here, Harper!" McKenzy gasps.

He jerks her backward, and she winces. I'm going to remember that when I'm twisting his balls off. "Quiet, bitch! Come this way, Harper. We can't do a proper exchange from way over there."

Without hesitation, I walk over so I'm just three feet in front of McKenzy. "Let her go."

I step forward, and Jack gives her a shove. As she stumbles past me, I press the car keys into her hand. "It's parked by that mansion," I hiss. "Now get the fuck out of here!"

"Harper!" she protests, but he shoots the ground right at her feet and she jumps back with a shriek.

"You heard her. Fuck off," he snarls, gesturing toward the door with his gun.

With one last pleading look, she runs out the door. A few moments later, I hear the car peel away.

"Now, before she gets the police involved," Jack drawls, grabbing my arm. "I think we should make our escape. Don't you?"

"Or you could just let me go and get out of here before you're implicated for two kidnappings." I'd run, but he has a gun on me. The wild look in his eyes tells me he's not stable enough for me to trust him.

He comes at me, grabbing me by the arm, and then drags me out of the creamery to a blue truck parked on the street.

So, the asshole was smart enough not to bring his own car. Damn. He pushes me into the passenger seat. I immediately lock the doors. As he's walking around the other side of the truck, I scramble around, checking the visor and the glove compartment for keys. Maybe there's a spare set and I can drive away.

Jack uses a fob to open the driver's door and laughs at my antics. He dangles the keys at me. "Looking for this?"

I bare my teeth at him. "Fucker."

"We'll get to that later." He grins. Then he slides behind the wheel, and we take off.

Now I look around for anything I can use as a weapon.

"I love you, Harper, but don't get cute. I'm not above doing a murder-suicide," he warns, glancing at me.

My stomach turns. "You don't love me, Jack. People don't kidnap someone if they love them."

"Really? You're going to try to appeal to my better nature? I killed an impound lot attendant to get this truck," he reveals. "I do love you, Harper. And you're going to be mine forever, one way or another. So I suggest you get used to the idea."

"I'm never going to get used to the idea. No matter what you have in mind, I'll never willingly stay with you, Jack. You'll end up killing me in the end, if the hundreds of people looking for us can't find us."

Jack points the gun at my temple while he drives one-handed. "Be careful what you wish for, Harper."

Trembling with fear, I still turn my head so the gun's pointed at my forehead and look him right in the eyes. "Do it." I know he won't.

His eyebrows draw together in confusion. He lowers the gun. "You are one crazy bitch, Harper Ward."

I look down at the gun in his hand, now pointed at the gear shift, and am just about to make a grab for it when Jack's phone rings. He holsters the gun and picks up his phone.

"Yeah?" he barks into it. "What the fuck do you mean, they've picked up McKenzy? How did they even find her?!"

A tickle of laughter goes through me. Damien. God bless him.

"Shut up!" Jack shouts at me. "No, not you," he says into the phone. "Shit. A tracker? In the car?"

Instead of stopping, my laugh becomes hysterical. "You are so dead, Jack Collins."

He glares at me, a hint of speculation in his eyes. "I'll call you back."

Suddenly, we careen into a cornfield. "Take your shirt off," he orders.

I snort. "No."

He frowns. "Take it off, Harper, or I'll do it for you."

Well, given that option… I scowl and pull my shirt over my head.

Jack grabs it and tosses it out his window. He does the same with my pants, shoes, and socks.

"What?" I ask when he's still glaring at me in my underwear.

"Gotta make sure there's no trackers in your clothes."

Damien wouldn't have gone that far. Then again, I wouldn't put it past him to suggest I get a tracker in my IUD the next time I'm due. It makes me chuckle. "Fuck you, Jack."

He pulls out a pocket knife, and I back to the door, trying the handle, but it's locked. He grabs me by the arm and pulls me toward him.

"Stop it!" I protest, kicking at him.

He pins my leg under his arm, trying to check there are not trackers in my underwear. I drag my fingernails down his cheek.

Jack hisses. "Bitch!"

I lean back to kick him with my other leg when my elbow hits the window button. Surprisingly, he never thought of putting the window lock on. Triumph!

I'm so focused on getting the window down that I don't see him grab something else until there's a sting in my ass.

"What the f—?" I blink a few times. The world is swimming before my eyes.

"You are a real pain in the ass, Harper Ward," Jack grunts, letting go of my leg.

I might be drifting off, but I use my last wisps of consciousness to kick him in the balls.

* * *

I WAKE up in the bed of the truck. The cover is on, so I might as well be stuck in a trunk. It's pitch black, and I'm bouncing painfully against the plastic liner as Jack drives us God knows where.

I'm not naked, though, which is a plus. I run my hands over my body and find he's dressed me again, which is a good thing. It doesn't feel as though he's violated me either, which is a huge relief.

After gathering all that silent info, I bounce-crawl to the end of the truck bed and feel around for the lift gate release. Of course, Jack has disabled the release somehow. I'm stuck.

I kick up against the cover next and just end up hurting my feet. The smell of dirt fills my nostrils and, with the bumping, I decide we must be on a dirt road. I don't know how long we stay on it, but it feels like a long time.

When we stop, I poise myself to leap out of the truck. Instead, Jack leaves the cover down.

"Leg," he orders me.

"Fuck you!" I reply. How did he even know I was awake?

"You kicked the cover pretty hard," he answers without my asking. "You must be in pain. Give me your leg."

"You're just going to inject me again," I accuse him. "You're not worried about my pain."

Jack smacks the cover, making me jump. "Harper, I'm going to leave you in there to die of heat stroke if you don't stick your leg out right now. Do you know what it's like to die of broiling to death in a metal box?"

That doesn't sound pleasant to me. I'm already hot and sweating, I realize. I'd been so focused on getting out that I hadn't even noticed before.

With a sigh, I stick my leg out of the back of the truck.

"Good girl," he muses.

"Only Damien gets to call me tha—" I begin, cut off as I feel a pinch. My vision swims.

"You son of a bitch," I groan before I pass out again.

TWENTY-FIVE

Love Slaps

Two hours earlier…

SCOTT

"This isn't right," Damien says.

I look at him in the rearview mirror. "What's not right?"

"She stopped in Hastings, but now she's heading back to the city, as far as I can tell." He leans back to show me his phone. "I can't believe they didn't catch her when she stopped. Technical difficulties. God, these boondock towns…"

"You know Vermillion is a suburb of Hastings, right?" I remark dryly.

"I stand by what I said." He turns to Tomás. "We need to head toward West St. Paul."

I grab the oh-shit bar as Tomás makes a one-eighty on two wheels, causing a lot of honking. Then we're speeding away from Hastings on Highway 55.

"She's on 494 West. Where on earth is she going?" Damien mutters.

"That's not the highway I'd take to get back to the apartment, unless I was taking a really, really long way around," Tomás chimes in, equally confused.

"McKenzy's parents live in West St. Paul," Rafe clarifies for everyone. "Maybe she's taking McKenzy home?"

"Ohh," the rest of us say. Did she actually get McKenzy free from Jack?

Damien puts his phone to his ear and begins giving clipped orders to someone. It could be the president, for all I know. He seems like the kind of guy to have that kind of power. He ends the call abruptly then turns to all of us. "The West St. Paul police are picking her up as we speak."

"Good," Rafe says. "Thank God we got her before she did something stupid."

Damien's phone shrills just as Rafe's last word dies on the air. "What?" Damien demands. He frowns, then scowls. "Fine. We'll be there shortly." He hangs up and tosses the phone angrily on the floor in front of him. "It's not Harper."

"It's not Harper?" I echo. "Who's in her car then?"

"McKenzy. She was so hysterical she grabbed a cop and started shaking him. His partner got a little taser-trigger happy and almost tazed her." Damien makes a noise of disgust. "I can't *fucking* believe this!"

"Where is Harper?" Tomás asks anxiously.

"I don't know." Damien has lost all of his usual cool and punches the dashboard.

"*¡Oye!* Be nice to Magdalena," Tomás snaps.

Damien shakes his head. "I swear I am getting her chipped."

"Stalker," Rafe says, but there's no malice in it. In truth, if she did have a chip, life would be a lot easier right now.

"They took McKenzy to the West St. Paul police station. We'll be able to see her there." Damien looks down at the floor where he threw his phone. "Fuck."

I take my phone out and program in the address, handing it to the front. "Here. This'll get us there."

Tomás drops the phone in a cup holder, and we follow the

robotic, completely unruffled voice to the West St. Paul police station.

While the voice is calm, all of us are rattled to the bone by the time we get to our destination. Rafe jumps out of the car while it's still moving. Damien isn't far behind him.

"You can't even wait for me to park?" Tomás complains, but after he gets the car into a spot, he also sprints toward the police station doors.

I take up the rear as Rafe slams open the doors, hitting them like he's taking down a linebacker.

The desk sergeant looks up as we all enter. "Can I help you?"

"McKenzy Jasper," Damien says in a tone that a smart man would know not to argue with.

The desk sergeant is not a smart man. "I'm afraid she's being interviewed right now in connection to a kidnapping. Unless you're her lawyer, you can't see her."

Damien snaps his fingers at Rafe and holds out his hand.

At first, Rafe looks annoyed, then puzzled, then realizes that Damien wants his phone. He hands it over.

Damien punches in a number and puts the phone to his ear. "Fred, it's Damien. I'm at the station, and the desk sergeant is giving me a hard time…"

"Why does McKenzy need a lawyer?" I ask the desk sergeant.

"That's none of your busi—" The desk sergeant begins to shut me down, but then the phone on his desk rings. He holds up a finger for me to wait, then grabs the handset. "Hello? Sir?" He pales. "Er… yes, sir. Four of them." He looks at Damien. "Mr. Blackwood?"

"Yes, that's me. These are my associates, and I would very much also like to know why McKenzy needs a lawyer," Damien replies evenly.

We all face the desk sergeant with our arms folded over our chests.

"Well, I-I mean, she assaulted a cop…" the desk sergeant stutters. "She was driving recklessly without a proper ID, and she might be an accessory to kidnapping…"

Damien's steady gaze makes the desk sergeant shrink into himself. I'd give my left nut to have that kind of effect on people like that asshole behind the desk.

"I see. Fred, I'm going to have to let you go. I'll see you in Vail in a month. It's on me. You've been so helpful, thank you." Damien ends the call, then makes another, the desk sergeant's eyes widening more and more with fear with each tap of a number. "Cliff, I'm going to need you to come to the West St. Paul police station. Yes, there's a complete clusterfuck going on here, and I'm going to need you to get a nice young lady out of trouble. Oh, and file some assault charges and whatever else you can come up with, I'm sure she can give you the details. Thanks."

"Would you like to see Miss Jasper now?" the desk sergeant squeaks.

"Very much so, yes. She might be the only person who knows the location of Harper Ward, who has doubtless been kidnapped. Oh, and Miss Jasper was a kidnapping victim herself. If I find she's been badgered or abused in any way, everyone in this station will be scrubbing my mansion floors with a toothbrush by the end of the week," Damien growls.

"I've seen his house in *Architectural Digest*. That's a lot of floors," Rafe adds, leaning on the counter.

The desk sergeant gulps and hurriedly opens the door for us. "Please, come in. I'll just… I'll… um… I'll ask them to… uh… stop the interview until her lawyer gets here."

"You do that," Damien seethes.

* * *

HARPER

When I wake up, my arms are tingling and my wrists hurt. I turn my head, my temples throbbing with the movement. My wrists are cuffed to a wrought iron headboard.

I look down. I'm on a bed. I don't feel any signs that he's touched me, so that's good. My mouth and cheek hurt like a bitch, which isn't great, but it could be worse. It could be so much worse.

Is it going to get worse?

I push the thought away. That kind of defeatist thinking is just going to kill my morale. And I'm going to need as much of that as I can muster to get myself through this situation.

"You're awake."

I snap my head in the other direction and see Jack sitting on a dilapidated old floral chair next to the bed. "No thanks to you."

"You're a real firecracker, Harper. I've always liked that about you," he chuckles. Then he sobers. "But you need to get things straight in your head. I'm a man. I'm your man. And you're my woman, and you will do what I say from now on."

"You're a sadistic bastard," I grunt back, tugging on the cuffs. He's put them on pretty tight. I don't have enough room to wiggle my hands out.

"I wouldn't talk to me like that if I were you." He stands and walks over to the bed.

I shift as far away from him as I can with my hands cuffed where they are.

He trails his fingertips down my smarting cheek. "You'll learn to love me again. You'll see. We're going to be very happy together."

"You're insane," I tell him. "What are you going to do, beat it into me?"

"All's fair in love and war," he replies.

"You know what? That murder-suicide thing is looking better and better by the minute."

Jack shakes his head. "I'll go get you some water."

My throat is parched, but I'm not drinking anything he hands me. I'm not that desperate. Besides, what if I need to use the bathroom? Will he insist on watching me?

Gross.

He comes back with the water and holds the glass to my lips. I take some in my mouth and spit it in his face.

"Bitch!" He grips my chin and forces my mouth open, pouring the water down my throat. I either have to swallow or choke to death, and I'm not quite ready to give up on an escape yet, so I swallow.

"Better," he growls, releasing my jaw. "There aren't going to be any fucking water or hunger strikes in this house."

"I hope you die," I cough. "I hope Damien kills you."

Jack glares at me, murder in his eyes. "Don't you *dare* say any of their names in front of me!"

"Fuck you!" He pushes my head, and it smacks against the wrought iron. It makes me see stars, but I'm not going to give him the satisfaction of knowing he's caused me pain.

"Stubborn as a mule," he mutters, stepping away from the bed. "Stop making me hurt you, Harper. You've got to get your mouth under control before I lose my shit."

"Fuck you," I repeat.

He scowls and raises his hand again. I brace myself.

His phone rings.

Jack stops himself and pulls his phone out of his jeans pocket instead. "Hey, man, thanks for calling. What's the update?"

Someone is helping this asshole? I strain to hear what's being said, but the words are too garbled.

"You told them McKenzy's an accessory to kidnapping?" He laughs at whoever's on the other end. "That's great! I wouldn't have thought of that myself. Genius."

Shit. Is McKenzy in some sort of legal trouble now? "You leave McKenzy alone!" I yell.

"Just a second." He lowers the phone to his chest. "Shut up. Nobody wants to hear your yapping."

"I'm telling you, if you've done anything to McKenzy..." I warn.

"You're going to what? Report me to the police?" He chuckles and pats me on the head in a belittling manner. "That's cute."

I bite his hand.

"Fuck!" He yanks his hand back and balls it into a fist, shaking it at me with a murderous look in his eyes. I brace myself again, but he just goes back to his phone conversation. "Yeah, Harper's being a pain in the ass. Don't worry. I've got it all under control."

He hangs up and shakes his head. "You know, you make me so

mad, Harper. I wouldn't hit you if you'd just be a good girl for me. A good wife. You're the one bringing this on yourself."

"I can't believe they ever let you be a cop," I scoff. "Oh, wait, I think *Damien* took care of that problem already, didn't he?"

Jack growls but doesn't touch me this time. Maybe I'm bruised enough for his taste. "I'm going to go watch some TV. You can just stay here and think about how you want your future to be. You're going to have lots and lots of time to think while you're with me." He stomps out of the room.

I fight the handcuffs, the bed shaking and creaking as I struggle. My wrists become bloody and raw, but I don't make any progress. The wrought iron loops I'm cuffed to are closed, so I can't slip them off the curlicues. No matter how hard I pull, nothing bends.

Finally, I give up, for now, and listen to the television. Maybe I'll hear my name. My men must have raised the alert by now.

Twenty minutes after *Wheel of Fortune* ends, I hear my name as the top story on the news. "...Thought to have been kidnapped by this man, Jack Collins."

Jack swears, and I hear a crash, then a shatter. Since the TV is still going, I assume something else fell victim to his wrath.

I smile and sit back on the bed.

It's only a matter of time, I tell myself.

TWENTY-SIX

Questioning McKenzy

Tomás

Damien gets us into the interview room where two flustered detectives sit in front of a completely shell-shocked McKenzy.

"Mr. Blackwood, this is highly unusual," one of them is enough of an *idiota* to say.

Rafe snorts. Scott shakes his head.

I just wait.

Damien turns on the detective and strikes like a viper with his words. "And I'm hoping you like early retirement."

"What the hell does that mean?" the detective snaps back. He's puffed up and stupid. Damien is going to eat him for breakfast.

I let the other two watch the show. I'm more concerned about McKenzy. She looks like she's on the last thread of her last frayed nerve. I go and kneel by her chair. "McKenzy?" I ask softly.

Now that I'm able to see under the table, I realize that her hands are cuffed together. Anger rises in me.

"Who has the fucking key?" I ask, standing abruptly.

"Key?" Rafe asks. "What do you mean, 'who has the key'?"

Scott looks at me, looks at McKenzy, leans down a little so he can see under the table, and stands back up completely red-faced. "She's cuffed."

Damien stops his banter with the detective, holding up a hand to silence the man. The detective gapes at Damien, clearly unable to fathom the gall he must have to give him such a gesture. "I'm sorry, repeat that please?"

"She's cuffed," Scott repeats, his lip curling with disgust.

"Ah, one moment." Damien turns back to the detective. "Pardon my reach."

Even my jaw drops when Damien suddenly grabs the detective by the shirtfront and shakes him. "Where," Damien asks dangerously, "is the fucking key to the handcuffs?"

"You can't—" the detective splutters.

The other detective reaches over his partner with a key in his outstretched palm. "Give it up, Norm. If you want to do a dick-measuring contest with one of the richest men in America, be my guest, but I like my job, thank you very much."

Rafe snatches up the key and hands it to me. "Uncuff her, Tomás."

"With pleasure." I kneel back down by McKenzy and undo the cuffs. I drop them on the floor with a clank and massage her wrists. "Can you tell us what happened, McKenzy? Did Jack hurt you?"

"H-He took Harper," McKenzy tells us, her voice trembling. "Harper came. I told her not to. He let me go and took her."

"Yes, I know that's your story, but we have it on good authority that this woman was an accessory to the kidnapping," Norm sneers.

Damien changes his grip from Norm's shirt to his throat and squeezes. "Who is this 'good authority'?"

Norm chokes, his eyes bulging.

"Um… Damien… that might be overstepping just a little bit…" Rafe says with a wince, putting a hand on Damien's shoulder.

Damien doesn't let go. "Who?"

McKenzy rubs her wrists, which are red and raw.

"Squeeze harder," I tell Damien without one bit of hesitation.

The other three look back at me, and it's clear she was hand-cuffed way too tight.

Rafe takes his hand off Damien's arm.

"Look, Norm didn't do it, okay?" the other detective pleads. "It was one of the arresting officers. Mr. Blackwood, I know my partner's an idiot. I also know you could probably kill him right here in front of me and the whole world would hear it was self-defense. But I'd consider it a personal favor if you'd not choke him to death."

Damien glances at him. "The cost of that is the name of the person who said McKenzy was an accessory to kidnapping. She wasn't, and you have treated her quite poorly from arrest to interrogation. I am going to have my men so far up your ass you'll be spitting their shoelaces for the rest of your career."

The detective winces. "His name is Sergeant Steve Keller. Now please, let Norm go."

Damien releases Norm. I can't help but feel a small wave of disappointment as Norm sits back, coughing and gasping for air, but then, Norm's partner is right. Norm didn't cause the damage to McKenzy's wrists.

"McKenzy," I say kindly, turning my attention back to Harper's distressed best friend. "Do you know where he was taking her? What he was driving?"

"J-Jack said he k-killed an impound lot at-tendant." McKenzy's teeth chatter as she speaks. "I should have followed them, but I was so scared. And Jack threw my phone out the truck window after he grabbed me. I was just trying to go home." She bursts into tears. "I want to go home, Tomás."

"I know, sweetie. I know," I reply, hugging her to me and rubbing her back. "We'll get you home as soon as we can. To your parents' house, right?"

"Yes. Please." She pauses, then her eyes get wide with horror. "Are they all right?!"

I squeeze her tighter because it feels like she's about to come apart. "*Sí*, McKenzy. Your parents were just knocked unconscious with a drug. They are fine now. Worried about you, I'm sure." I glare at Norm.

"Did you call her parents?" Scott asks before Damien can.

"Uh…" Norm rubs his neck and watches Damien cautiously. "Um… we might have… not… done that yet."

"I'm supposing McKenzy hasn't gotten her phone call yet," Damien adds icily.

"She didn't ask!" Norm argues.

"Here, darling. This is Rafe's phone." Damien presses it into her hands. "You go ahead and call your parents, and Tomás will drive you home."

McKenzy looks at the phone and bites her lip. "What about Harper?"

"We're going to make sure she gets home too," Damien reassures her. "You've done so well, McKenzy. You just let us take care of it from here on out, okay? You need to go home and be with your parents."

She sniffles, then nods. "Okay." She dials her parents' number.

I can hear her father answer with a sharp, "Who is this?"

McKenzy's voice cracks and she cries fresh tears. "Daddy?"

"We still need to ask her some questions, and she needs to sign some paperwork. And—" The other detective begins ticking things off on his fingers.

"I think that can wait, don't you?" Damien asks. It's not a question.

The detective gulps. "Absolutely, sir."

After a few minutes on the phone with her parents, McKenzy is able to collect herself. "It's a blue truck," she tells us. "It's a blue truck with one of those truck bed covers."

"*Bueno*, McKenzy. Good job," I respond, holding her hand.

"I think we need to have a word with this Steve Keller person," Damien muses. "He might have a lot to tell us."

"He's at home," Norm says, finally clued in to the fact that he wants to be as helpful to Damien as possible.

"I require an address and an armed escort," Damien replies with the same offhand expectation as if he'd just asked to use the restroom.

Norm swallows. "Yes, sir."

* * *

HARPER

Evening turns to night. Even though the curtains are drawn over the small bedroom window, there's still enough light around and through the fabric to be able to tell that much. As the minutes stretch and time crawls along, I hear the TV finally go off.

Jack comes into the bedroom, pulling at the buttons on his shirt. "Bedtime."

I scowl at him. "What do you mean 'bedtime'?"

"You know what I mean." He grins, taking off his shirt, then his pants, leaving him in boxers.

I lock my legs together. He's not getting any of this.

He laughs. "I'm not going to force you, babe. But there is only one bed, and I am sleeping there."

"Fantastic." My voice drips sarcasm. "What a lucky girl I am."

Jack shrugs and comes over to the bed. He uncuffs one of my wrists from the headboard, then slaps the cuff over his own wrist, tethering me to him. "Need the bathroom before bed?" he asks.

Yes. But I'd rather wet the bed than go into the bathroom with you. "Nope."

"Liar. But hey, if you want to hold it all night, that's your prerogative." He gets in bed next to me, shoving me to one side with his hip.

I lie very still, not wanting even the slightest twitch of my body to seem like any kind of encouragement to him. Still, he wraps himself around me and lays his head on my shoulder, nuzzling in close.

Bile rises in my throat.

"This is the way it should be." He sighs, happy as a clam while I want to projectile vomit all over him. "Just like this."

I don't comment. If I make him mad, he might change his mind about forcing me. If I don't make him mad, whatever I say might be taken as some form of encouragement.

"Goodnight, Harper."

He yawns and is soon snoring, but I'm wide awake. My whole body feels gross now, my wrists hurt, and I desperately need to pee.

I wonder if I should wake him up and demand he cuffs me in a more comfortable position. Then it dawns on me.

Jack has the key.

Jack has the key close enough to unlock the cuffs.

I glance over him in the lamplight at the bedside table on his side, but the key isn't there. That can only mean…

Hope blossoms in my chest and I look down at his boxers. They have a pocket in them.

Bingo.

I barely dare to breathe as I wriggle our joined hands down. Jack was always a deep sleeper, thank God. I feel around the pocket on the hip that's thrown over mine, carefully avoiding his erection. Just the idea of touching it, even by accident, makes my skin crawl. My fingers brush against a small, hard bit of metal. I could cry with joy. If he'd hidden it away on the other side, there would have been no possible way for me to reach it. Now, I slip my fingers into his pocket and draw out the key. Jack just keeps snoring.

I maneuver my hand so the cuffs are pinned beneath my wrists. I can't unlock myself, but there's just enough give, if I bite my lip against the pain, to unlock him. I do so, then slide the cuff off his wrist. The metal cuffs dangle from my wrist as I wiggle out from under him. I bring my hand up to uncuff myself from the headboard and the metal clangs against the wrought iron bars. I freeze.

He grumbles in his sleep and rolls onto his side away from me.

Resolving to be more careful, I wait for the cuffs hanging off my wrist to stop swinging, then reach up to unlock myself.

I don't even bother taking the one set of cuffs off me. I simply spring from the bed and tiptoe out the door. I close it quietly behind me.

Wherever this place is, it's completely unfamiliar to me. Jack has never brought me here before, I'm sure of it. Pictures are spaced around here and there of people I don't know, telling me this place probably isn't even his.

I go to the front door and find that it's locked and requires a key to unlock it. Stifling a groan of frustration, I press my forehead against the warm wood. As with the handcuffs, even from the inside, I can't unlock this door without a key.

Heaving a sigh, I hunt around for another option. I find a bathroom with a window that's cracked part way open and decide to kill two birds with one stone. I quickly relieve myself then shove the window the rest of the way up.

It makes the loudest scraping noise I've ever heard in my life.

"Shit, shit, shit!" I hiss.

A door slams open somewhere else inside the house. "HARP-ER?!" Jack roars.

There's no going back now. I stand on the toilet and launch myself out the window and onto the ground below.

TWENTY-SEVEN

Allies and Assholes

Rafe

Tomás promises to rejoin us after we shake the Steve Keller tree. McKenzy really needs to go home, poor thing. Jack Collins is getting the ass kicking of a lifetime once we find him.

Norm knocks on Keller's door while Damien stands patiently behind him. There are some bewildered police officers outside behind us. I suppose they aren't used to having to put the pressure on one of their own.

A second knock finally brings Keller to the door. He looks at the whole lot of us outside, especially at Norm, and frowns. "What?" he demands.

Damien's lips tighten. I understand. I don't like his tone either.

"Mr. Keller?" Damien asks coldly.

"Yeah? Who's asking?" Keller grumps.

"Damien Blackwood. I think you've been a bit of an asshole, Mr. Keller," Damien says.

Norm finds his balls and talks over Damien. "We just want to know where Harper Ward is, Steve. I'm sure Jack lied to you. He kidnapped one girl and traded her for Miss Ward. He killed an impound attendant. He stole a truck from the impound. He's in a lot of trouble, and we think Miss Ward is in grave danger."

"I think you should have led with the fact he killed someone already," Scott grumbles.

"I agree," I add.

Keller pales a bit, then shrugs. "I don't know what that has to do with me."

My hands ball into fists.

"Rafe, please. I need you to be in tip-top shape for my Fantasy Football roster," Damien says before I can slug the lying bastard. His eyes turn cold, and his smile is scary enough to make a smart man's dick shrivel up and die.

Like Norm, Steve is not a smart man. He might be even dumber.

"Were you going to let him hit a cop? Look, I don't care who you are, Maloney. Hitting a cop has serious consequences. I think you should all step off my doorstep and go about your business." Keller snorts, starting to close the door.

Damien slips one patent leather shoe into the doorway, preventing it from closing. Keller was closing it pretty hard, but if it hurt at all, Damien doesn't let on. "I'm rather disappointed in you, Mr. Keller. An intelligent individual would know when he's been caught and would be doing everything he could to save his badge right now."

"Don't you threaten me, Blackwood. You ain't the shit either," Keller scoffs.

Scott cracks his knuckles. "I don't usually believe in violence, but…"

Damien waves a hand. "No need for that, Scott. No, I've got this all under control." He looks over at Norm. "Don't I, Norm?"

Norm swallows. "Captain says we have to arrest you if you don't start talking, Steve. You're the one who suggested Miss Jasper was an accessory to kidnapping. We've since learned she was the victim. So you need to confess, or you're in some serious trouble."

"I convinced the captain that perhaps you deserved a second

chance, as long as you told us where Harper is," Damien continues, his tone glacial.

Keller turns to Norm, ignoring Damien. "I can't believe you'd hang a fellow cop out to dry like this."

"Steve. He *killed* someone. You really want to be an accessory to murder?!" Norm bellows.

I'd been wondering where that temper of his went. "Look, Steve," I chime in as he tries to toe Damien's unmoving foot out of his doorway. "I know you know you're in deep shit. Damien's offering you a get-out-of-jail-free card. You can be the hero of this situation, buddy. I can't imagine Jack told you he killed an impound lot attendant…"

"Fuck you, Maloney," Keller seethes. "You could all be lying to me. I do know Jack told me she's a whore, and as far as I can tell, she must be because there's three of you civilians standing here, asking me about her. Sometimes a woman needs to know her place."

My throwing hand is about to get more of a beating. I draw my fist back, rage burning all the way up to my eyeballs, but before I can deliver this guy his well-deserved attitude correction, Scott's fist flies past me and socks the asshole right in the jaw.

I end up having to grab Scott, with Norm, to keep him from diving on the bastard and pummeling him to death. I mean, I understand the sentiment, but…

"Scott, we need to know where Harper is," Damien scolds him. "That can't happen if Mr. Keller can't speak."

"Yeah, what he said," I say. Scott is really freakishly strong. Better than most linebacker I've come up against.

But then, he is a farm boy. "Come on, cool your jets." I grip him harder. "We're gonna get the information we need. Damien will remove his balls with a spork in front of God and everyone if he has to."

Scott growls but finally stops straining against our holds. "I get to use the spork," he grunts.

"Fair enough." Damien turns back to Steve, who is holding his jaw. "Now, you stupid, misogynistic waste of oxygen, where were we? Ah, yes. *Where* is Harper Ward?"

* * *

HARPER

Branches cut my face as I stumble through the darkness, the moon and stars my only light. I've tripped twice and scraped my hands, and they're throbbing now along with my wrists. So are my knees, my thighs, my calves, and my lungs.

What keeps me going is the crashing sound behind me, like I'm being chased by an angry bear. Light bounces behind me every time I look over my shoulder, and I know that asshole is carrying a flashlight, which I feel is an unfair advantage.

I trip again and this time go tumbling down an embankment. I land in a trickle of water, which must be a small stream.

There's a fallen tree over the stream, so I crawl over to it. I manage to get under the tree, my chest pressed into the water, my face straining just high enough for me to breathe.

Light shines around me, skimming the surface of the stream but not penetrating the darkness beneath the log.

"Harper!" Jack calls. "I'm not mad. I just think we need to talk. Let's go back to the cabin and forget all this silliness. You're just going to get hurt out here."

Fuck that shit. I don't make a sound. I'm even holding my breath.

He swears. There's a rustle, and I think he's walked away, but instead I hear a gunshot.

Something screams in the bushes.

"Fucking bitch," he mutters as he steps through the stream with a loud splash to go see what he shot.

I don't know what it is. I feel bad for it, but I'm also glad it wasn't me.

Not mad, my ass.

Whatever it is keeps screaming until he swears loudly again and lets off another shot. Then there's just silence except for the trickle of water and the crunch of his boots. He stomps off into the distance, leaving a quieting echo in his wake.

The stream splashes me in the face, but I decide this is as good a place to hide as any until morning where I can actually see where I'm going. It's cramped, uncomfortable, cold, and my new home until daylight.

Or so I think. A bullhorn makes a loud squeal through the darkness.

"Office Jack Collins, this is the police. We have you surrounded. Come out with your hands up!" a stern voice barks over the bullhorn.

That's great. The police have found me, but I'm in the fucking woods and not the cabin, which is what I'm sure they have 'surrounded.'

I strain to hear if Jack is coming back this way. My best bet now is to get to the safety of the police, and I know it.

Taking a deep breath, I crawl from under the fallen tree and out of the stream. I clench my jaw to keep my teeth from chattering. It's cool outside, fall rearing its ugly head just when I needed it to still be summer. I could have died of hypothermia before the sun rose.

Good thing the cops are here.

I make my way back up the embankment on my hands and knees, then stand and head toward the bright lights. The police must have floodlights on the cabin.

"Jack Collins!" the bullhorn voice booms again. "It's over. Come out with your hands up."

It's over.

Relief almost makes me stumble. I lean against a tree for support, my legs shaking.

It's over.

Then I hear the hammer of a gun cock back. I spin around to see Jack right in front of me, holding a gun to my head.

"Guess it's our time, babe," he says regretfully.

My heart stops. *No, this can't be the end!*

I think of Damien, wondering where he is. Damien was going to save me.

Or Scott.

Or Tomás.

Or Rafe.

My men. My perfect men.

"Jack, please, don't," I whisper, holding up my hands in a pleading gesture. "Please."

"I'm sorry, babe." He presses the gun to my forehead. "At least we're going together."

There's a rustle in the underbrush, and Jack swings the gun away from me. "What the f—"

The last thing I see before the gun goes off is Rafe launching himself at Jack in a flying tackle.

TWENTY-EIGHT

Shot

Harper

Rafe and Jack are on the ground. I don't know where the bullet went. I don't know if Rafe's been shot. Neither of them are moving.

I drop to my knees next to them. "Rafe? Rafe, honey? Rafe?!" I shake his shoulder.

Nothing.

I put my hand on his cheek and something warm and sticky coats my palm. "Help!" I scream. "Oh, God, he's bleeding! Somebody help!"

A multitude of boots come trampling through the woods, flashlights shining on us from all directions. Some police stand back with their guns drawn while others rush to Rafe's side.

"It's just a graze," one officer says, and I could pass out from relief. "He'll be okay. Just gotta get him in to see if he has a concussion. He's a football player though, so I suppose he's had a few of those."

Someone hits their knees next to me while I'm staring down at Rafe and wraps their arms tightly around me. I turn my head and see it's Tomás. "You're okay, Harper. It's over now."

This time, it really is. Rafe tackled Jack as the gun went off, and they both hit the ground so hard, Jack was knocked out. I'm not sure why Rafe isn't moving if it's just a graze. Maybe he hit his head. I start to tremble as I realize it's finally over.

Except that, even though his eyes are closed, Jack is reaching for the gun that had been knocked from his hand.

I open my mouth to say something, but a shiny leather shoe comes down hard on his wrist. Jack yelps.

"That's enough of that, fucker" Damien says, plucking the gun off the ground and handing it to one of the cops kneeling next to Rafe.

Jack tries to reach down to his own ankle, but the police officers glom onto the situation and remove his ankle piece as well. He howls in frustration.

Scott kneels down on my other side and hugs me so I'm sandwiched between two of my men. I try not to cry, but it's an impossible feat. Tears roll down my cheeks, and I cling to both of them.

I'm sobbing when the paramedics come down to get Rafe. Damien grinds his foot down on Jack's wrist. I hear a crack and Jack wails like a little girl. The cops move in and haul Jack off the ground while the paramedics tend to Rafe. I want to go to him, but Scott tells me I need to stay back. As much as I want to check on Rafe, he needs medical attention now. When they load him up to head to the hospital, I'm told he'll be fine.

"Let's go to the hospital, little red bird," Damien tells me, wrapping his arms around me. I hug him tightly and then move with him toward the house where I assume the vehicles are parked.

"Harper. Don't go. We're meant to be together," Jack whines from where they're hauling him way.

"You have the right to remain silent..." one of the cops reminds him.

"Harper!" Jack calls again.

I turn my back on him. "Let's go to the hospital," I agree.

As it happens, Scott and Tomás have to support me all the way back to the cabin. I see the ambulance and stop. "I think I should go with him."

"His ambulance already left," Damien tells me, reaching out to squeeze my hand. "That one's for you."

I can't believe I'm so out of it that I didn't notice an ambulance leave. My knees buckle and Scott scoops me up in his strong arms.

"Rafe would want you taken care of," Damien says. "And we're all coming with you." I don't argue.

Of course when we get to the ambulance, the EMTs are not so keen on letting three men ride with me. They help me onto a gurney and one of them starts assessing my wounds while the other addresses my men. "Are you family?"

"Yes," Damien replies without hesitation.

The EMT looks pointedly at Tomás, whose olive complexion makes him the least likely to be family to me. "Are you sure? And we can only take one of you anyway."

"We're family," he insists. "And we're all going in the ambulance. Got it?"

The EMT lets out a deep breath and then and steps back to allow all of them into the back of the ambulance.

"That's better," Damien muses, settling in across from me while Tomás and Scott take either side.

The EMTs treat my hands, my scraped palms and chafed wrists. I have a bump on my head where I hit it on the bed. I also have cuts and scrapes on my face from my run through the woods.

Tomás mumbles in a low tone. " I don't suppose there's any way to make Jack's stay in prison a little less… enjoyable?"

Damien's jaw tightens as his eyes darken with anger. "I'll look into it."

"Please don't bother," I say, my lip smarting with every word. "He's not worth it."

"Hmm," is Damien's only response.

I lean my head back and close my eyes. I'm so tired. I just want to go to sleep, but I ask, "I suppose you're going to find some poisonous mushroom and bake a cake for him, Scott?"

"I wouldn't bother with the cake," Scott grunts.

Tears sting my eyes. *My good, loyal men.* A tear trickles down my cheek, stinging the scratches even though they've been treated.

Scott's eyebrows draw together with concern. He looks so torn up about all of this. All of them do.

I look around at the three of my four men who are with me, and they appear to be in total agreement. "I don't know what to say," I sob.

"Say you won't do something this stupid ever again," Damien replies sternly.

"At least, not without us, *cariña*," Tomás says.

I nod. "Okay."

"Promise?" Damien presses.

"I promise."

The rest of the short ride to the hospital I close my eyes and let the EMTs treat me while I bask in the love of my men—all of them. I could never give up even a single one of them

Not now, not ever.

* * *

"I'M FINE. STOP FUSSING!" I say to the doctor who is stitching one of the worst cuts on my hand and wrapping my hands with gauze. "I want to see Rafe."

"Mr. Maloney is resting," the doctor replies, shaking her head at me. "And Mr. Blackwood told me we need to do an MRI of your head."

"An MR—ugh, that nervous Nellie. I'm fine. Really." I give my head a shake back and forth to show her, but it makes my vision swim.

"We're also doing a tox-screen. I managed to talk Mr. Blackwood out of a full-body scan. You're welcome," she adds.

I groan. "I'm sorry. He can be… a bit much."

"Look, we'll get you in for an MRI within about four hours. That will give Mr. Maloney some more time to sleep off the terrible headache I'm sure he has. He hit his head pretty hard, and his shoulder will take some time to heal," the doctor continues. "Members of his team and the team's medical staff are already here, insisting on a million different tests."

"And Damien isn't helping." I sigh.

"And Mr. Blackwood isn't helping. Well, he is. Just not an over-worked hospital. He's helping you and Mr. Maloney." She shrugs. "If I had that kind of power, I'd do the same for those close to me. I understand."

"I'm still really sorry." I wince as she places an icepack on my cheek.

"Hold this," she instructs me. "Once that area gets numb, move it to your other cheek. Alternate back and forth."

I glance around the room for a mirror. "How bad do I look?"

"This isn't a beauty contest.." The doctor cleans up her equipment, then starts heading for the door. "I'll let Mr. Blackwood, Mr. García, and Mr. Bauer in now."

"Great. As if I don't have enough people fussing over me," I complain.

The doctor snickers. "Consider yourself lucky. Some people who come in here have no one."

A concern pops into my head, and I quickly ask, "Has someone contacted Rafe's parents?"

"Yes. Mr. Maloney's next of kin are on their way," the doctor assures me. "Now, you get some rest until the MRI. You've had quite an ordeal."

I lean back on the bed as the three men come in, Damien pushing past the doctor to take the chair immediately at my bedside. "How are you feeling?"

"I'm fine, Damien. I promise," I assure him.

Scott and Tomás pull up chairs, Scott on my other side, Tomás next to Damien. They all look rather grim.

"Really, I'm okay," I insist, wondering what has them so down. "Did Jack escape or something?"

"No. That man isn't going anywhere but prison," Damien assures me.

"Then what?" I ask.

They all look at each other. Then Tomás blurts, "Damien called your parents, but they won't come."

My heart sinks. I didn't even think of them. I guess they didn't think of me either. Not after our last conversation. "Oh," is all I can manage.

Scott puts a hand on my arm. "We're your family now. Don't even worry about them. They're the ones missing out."

For the third time since my rescue, I start crying. "Sorry. God, what's with the waterworks? They were so insulting to me. That Melody is evil incarnate… I don't know why I'm crying."

"It's just hard, little red bird," Damien says softly, stroking my hair. He pulls a twig out of it with a fond smile. "You just concentrate on getting better."

"And cry all you want," Tomás adds. "We all understand."

They all nod.

I get choked up and wave at them all to come in for a group hug.

"I love you," I say fiercely once we're all squeezed together. "I love all of you so much."

"Good," Scott replies. "Because we love you too."

TWENTY-NINE

Up and About

Harper

After my MRI, the doctors finally let me go see Rafe. I shuffle down to his room in hospital socks and a gown. Tomás has gone to pick up some pizza for us all. Damien is on his phone, leaning on the technicians and whoever else is involved to get my MRI reviewed. Scott stepped out to call someone to check on his animals since he's been gone so long.

I knock lightly on the door to Rafe's room. When I hear Jen, Rafe's mother, call "Come in!" I push open the door and go inside.

Jen is sitting next to the bed, holding Rafe's hand. His father, Skip, is leaning against the windowsill with his arms folded. When they look up, neither of them are particularly happy to see me.

"Harper," Jen says in a clipped tone.

"Mrs. Maloney," I reply respectfully. "Mr. Maloney."

Skip eyes me with deep-seated anger.

"You could have ended his football career, you know?" Jen remarks, stroking Rafe's hair. He's sleeping soundly, which is good.

"I'm sorry. I should come back later." I can offer a million excuses, the first of which being I didn't *ask* him to tackle the gun-toting Jack, but I can feel the unwelcoming vibes rolling off both of them and think it would simply be best to remove myself from the situation.

Skip snorts. "Typical."

I frown at him. "I beg your pardon?"

"Running off when things get rough," he accuses me. "That's your MO, isn't it?"

"I was just going to give you all your privacy," I respond with failing politeness. "But if you have something you need to say to me, here I am."

"I can't believe you believed Melody over our Rafe all those years ago," Jen snaps. "He would never have slept with your friend! Don't you know how much our son loved you?"

"Still loves her," Skip grunts. "Even though she's whoring it around with Damien Blackwood."

My teeth grind against each other. "Actually," I say sweetly, "I'm 'whoring it around' with *three* other guys, not just Damien."

Jen gasps. "Harper!"

"I knew it," Skip sneers.

"So, yeah. Now that you've got your pound of flesh, I think I'll just—"

Skip stabs a finger in my direction. "I'm not *nearly* done with you, young lady!"

I should leave. I know I should leave. But I did let my psychopath friend convince me their son cheated on me with her. So, I stay to accept my lashings.

"You broke my son's heart. He nearly quit school and football because of you!" Skip shouts.

"I'm sorry about that. I believed my friend. I've learned better since then," I reply.

"Better? *Better?!* You let my son fall in love with you all over again, then go around behind his back—"

"Rafe knows," I interrupt him. "He knows about all three of them. And he still loves me."

Jen's jaw drops. "Excuse me?"

"And I love him. And I love them. And I know it's unconventional, and certainly not the kind of life I expected to be leading, but it is what it is. And yes, Melody is pure evil. She told me the truth herself about her and Rafe. Mocked me with it, even. I don't think my heart's ever been so shattered. Or that I've ever been so down on myself. But I can't fix what she did, or what I did, no matter how sorry I am. But I'm also not sorry about Damien, Scott, and Tomás any more than I'm sorry about Rafe. I'm not sorry about any of it," I add. "So, you're welcome to hate me like my parents do, but I'm not going to let you believe a bunch of untruths. There's been too much of that going around between Rafe and me."

"You…" Jen gapes. "You…you…"

"At least your parents disowned you," Skip scoffs.

I feel Skip's criticism more keenly than my parents'. I've always liked the Maloneys. They were going to be my in-laws. Now, everything is a crazy mess. But it's a mess that works for me and my men, so I can't apologize for it.

I can't think of anything to say to that.

"Dad, will you fucking shut up?" Rafe groans from the bed.

"Rafe!" Jen grabs her son's hand. "Darling, how are you feeling? Can you hear me? They said there might be permanent hearing damage from the gun going off…"

"I can hear you fine. Both of you. And I want you to lay off Harper," he grunts, struggling into a sitting position. He winces, and I know his head and shoulder must be killing him.

Jen ignores him. "We were just about to ask Harper to leave. I mean, obviously you know she's no good for you."

"I don't know that at all, Mom, and if you keep on her like that, you two are going to be the people who are no good for me," he growls.

"Rafe," I say quickly before the red-faced Skip can barge in. "It's okay. I just wanted to see if you were all right. We can talk later—"

"It's not okay and you're not going anywhere. I need to see that you're in one piece." He pulls his hand free of Jen's and gestures for me to come over to the bed.

I shuffle over in my socks and gown.

He tugs at the fabric. "Fashionable."

"I know, right? Versace is going to feature it in their next line," I quip.

Rafe looks up at my face and winces. "I'm sorry I wasn't there sooner, sugar."

"Hey, I'll take a couple of stitches in my hand to a hole in my head any day," I assure him, taking his hand and threading my fingers through his. "I'm just sorry you got mixed up with a bullet."

"I'd rather not do it again, but if I had to, I would," he murmurs, his gaze adoring.

I bite my lip.. "I love you. I don't want you to ever do that again."

"Son, if the media ever found out you were in a relationship with a woman who is dating three other men, they'd have a field day," Skip chimes in. "I can't believe you're risking so much for this trash."

"And you can leave. This 'trash' is my girlfriend, and I love her, and you two are the only ones making a big deal out of it. It's the twenty-first century. If anything, people are going to be intrigued. If they're not, fuck 'em. I don't need your negativity in my life, or theirs. It's *my* life," Rafe responds harshly.

"But…" Jen argues.

Rafe glares at her. "You two can wait outside. When I'm done with Harper, she can send you back in."

"Rafe, this is lunacy," his father says.

"And you're just worried about your allowance," he snaps.

"Rafe!" I object. "Don't say that to your parents!"

He turns to me with a sigh. "A lot has changed since I got famous, Harper. It's just the truth."

"Your father and I certainly don't just care about the money!" Jen cries.

"Key word being 'just,'" Rafe snorts.

Skip pushes himself away from the windows. "I'm not going to stand here and listen to this. Come on, Jen. Harper, don't bother getting us when you're done here. We won't be here."

"But, Skip…" Jen whimpers.

He glares at her. "Come along, Jen!"

She gets up, and Skip snatches her hand, pulling her out of the room.

"Rafe, I don't want to cause trouble between you and your parents. I know they love you," I say while the door is still reverberating in its frame from Skip slamming it.

He shakes his head. "Sugar, let's talk about something else." He sounds tired. No, world-weary. There's a lot more on his plate than just a bullet graze to the shoulder.

"Okay…" I sigh. "But you know I'm going to circle back to this later, right?"

"I know. Just not today." He pulls my hand to his lips and kisses the palm over the gauze. "I'm glad you're okay."

"Damien's having them rush an MRI analysis. Apparently, I needed my head examined," I joke.

Rafe laughs. "Yeah, me too. I was a bit out of it for a while there, but I did hear Damien barking orders at people. It must be his love language."

"Probably." I grin. I sit down on the edge of the bed and stroke his hair with my free hand. "Do you have a concussion?"

"Yeah, but not too bad. No disturbing brain bleeds or anything. I'll be up tossing the ball around before you know it," he tells me. "The shoulder's fine, too. Just a graze and not my throwing arm."

"I'm not worried about football. I'm worried about you," I murmur, combing my fingers through his hair, letting the strands slip between them.

He smiles at me, and it could have lit up the whole hospital. "Thanks, sugar. That's exactly how I felt when I jumped at him. He was going to shoot you."

"He shot you," I remind him. "That's not exactly something I'm happy about."

Rafe shrugs. "He only shot me a little bit."

"Can you only be a 'little bit' shot? Is that like being a 'little bit' pregnant?"

He pales. "Are you trying to tell me something?"

"No!" I shake my head vehemently. "God, no! IUD, remember?"

With a long sigh, Rafe lays back down. "Whew. You scared me for a minute there. I mean, I just became part of a quadruple. I'm not sure I'm ready to be a dad too."

I almost bite my lip again, but stop myself. "Is our... you know... four-way relationship really going to cause problems for your career?"

He shrugs. "Not any more than it will for Damien. I'm a little worried about Tomás, him being a professor and all, but it's not like he's teaching young kids. I don't think the parents can get too up in arms."

"Oh." I hadn't even thought of that. "I suppose Scott's the only one who's safe. And me. They kind of expect artists to have weird, convoluted sex lives."

"Do you think our sex lives are weird and convoluted?" he asks softly.

His blue eyes see right into my soul, so I hope he knows I mean it when I say, "No, I don't think they are."

"Good. Me neither." He presses my hand to his cheek. "We're all going to make this work. Because I'm sure we all love you, Harper. And you wouldn't be the you we love without all of us."

I give that some thought. "That's true. I love you, too."

THIRTY

Changes

Two weeks later…

HARPER

"WHOOOOOO! GO RAFE, GO!" I scream from the private suite where we are watching Rafe's game.

"Maybe we're supposed to call him Bullet?" Tomás asks, eating off a plate of catered food next to me.

"I figure if you're sleeping with the man, you get to call him whatever you want," Damien says dryly. He sips something expensive—scotch, I'm assuming—from a tumbler, but loses all sophistication when Rafe gets sacked. "Roughing the passer!"

"They can't flag the play every time Rafe gets sacked. This isn't touch football," Scott chuckles. He's munching popcorn, more a fan of that snack than the buffet fare.

Damien purses his lips. "I wonder how much it would cost…"

I reach past Tomás to slap his shoulder. "Don't even think about it."

He shrugs. "I'm just saying." His phone rings, and he frowns at the ID. "Excuse me."

While Damien is gone, Rafe throws a perfect spiral to a wide receiver for a touchdown. The Vikings take the lead.

Scott stands, popcorn dumping right out of his lap and onto the suite floor as the kicker makes the extra point "GO VIKES, YEAAH!"

We all clap enthusiastically.

Damien returns, his expression unreadable.

"Man, you missed a *hell* of a play!" Scott says, pounding Damien on the back. "Look, it's late in the fourth quarter, and we're winning the game!"

"Hmm." Damien looks at Rafe and his expression becomes troubled.

"What's wrong?" I ask, trying to keep one eye on the game. But when Damien has that look on his face, it almost always spells some kind of disaster.

"That was a friend of mine," he says quietly. "He just put a trade through for his football team and called to brag about it."

I can tell by the way he's talking this is something important. "What is it?"

We all stare at him.

He lets out a deep breath. "I probably shouldn't say anything since he doesn't know about it himself yet, but Rafe is going to be heading to San Francisco, Damien explains.

"What? No…" I shake my head. "No! Come on, we just got this thing working!"

"I tried to negotiate, but the owner stood firm. I don't know what he's being paid or who's blackmailing him, but Rafe is being traded. And there's nothing I can do about it." It's the last part that bothers Damien the most, I know. After making his billions, he's been used to getting his own way.

I look down at the field as Rafe slaps asses and bumps helmets with the rest of his team. "Does Rafe know yet?"

"No." Damien's jaw works. "They haven't told him yet."

"Maybe he'll retire?" Tomás suggests. "I mean, he must have quite a bit of money by now."

We all look at Tomás.

"He's too young to retire," Scott says.

"He really loves the game. This is going to crush him, either way." I sigh.

"My thoughts exactly." Damien takes a deep breath. "Well, of course you know I will fly all of us down to San Francisco periodically, especially you, little red bird."

"That's… that's very generous of you, Damien," I murmur. "I just want Rafe to make the decision that works best for him."

Damien pats my hand. "You won't have to give him up. We'll make this work. We're a family now."

"Okay." I look around at my men, then put my arms out for a group hug.

The rest of the game is miserable. Damien offers to break the news to Rafe before he gets blindsided, which I think is a good idea, but I still hate that this is happening to Rafe.

The Vikings win the game. I guess this is what it feels like to win the battle, but not the war.

When Rafe comes to meet us at Damien's place after the game, he's grinning from ear to ear. He sees how somber we are and frowns. "What? You didn't see we won?"

"Rafe, I think you'd better sit down," I suggest, patting the couch between Damien and me.

His frown deepens. "Please don't tell me you really are pregnant."

I roll my eyes. "Oh, my God, Rafe. I'm not pregnant!"

Rafe lets out a long whoosh of breath. "Okay." He sits down between us and glances from me to Damien and back again.

Scott is sitting across from us next to Tomás, a sympathetic expression on his face. Tomás has his professor face on. The one he gets when he has to tell a student bad news about their grade.

"Rafe," Damien begins, clearing his throat. "You're being traded to San Francisco. I'm sorry. There's nothing I can do. I've tried."

Rafe takes that in for a long moment. "I'm sorry, what?"

"You're being traded to the Forty-Niners," Damien repeats patiently. "Right before the trade deadline ends."

His mouth opens. Closes. Opens again. Then Rafe turns to me. "What are we going to do now?"

I don't know, but I'm certain I will find a way to keep my men with me. One way or another.

Thank you for reading! Book 2 is coming soon! In the meantime, please check out my other books on the next page. :)

Also by Sadie Waters

Chosen by the Princess: A Reverse Harem Romance,

Realm of the Chosen Book 1

Loved by the Princess: A Reverse Harem Romance,

Realm of the Chosen Book 2

Ruled by the Princess: A Reverse Harem Romance,

Realm of the Chosen Book 3

Realm of the Chosen: The Complete Series

Demon Seer: Ember's Flames Book 1

Demon Hunter: Ember's Flames Book 2

Demon Slayer: Ember's Flames Book 3

Queen of Winter

Follow me on social media!

Instagram: https://www.instagram.com/sadiewaters/

Facebook: https://www.facebook.com/sadiewatersauthor

Twitter: https://twitter.com/SadieWatersBook

Bookbub: https://www.bookbub.com/authors/sadie-waters